Eighty and Out

a novel by
Kim Cano

ISBN-10: 1508700656
ISBN-13: 978-1508700654

For Mom and Aunt Kathy.

Prologue

Back in the fifties, when my younger sister Jeannie and I were kids, we made a pact not to live past age eighty.

We'd seen our fair share of old people doddering around, struggling to make it from point A to point B with their walkers, and decided that wouldn't happen to us. We'd live life to the fullest and leave this planet with our dignity intact.

As we grew up, the plan dissolved into a silly idea we'd had when we were young and naïve and knew little about life. But now that I'm an older woman, one who has grown wise in her years, I've given the pact more thought.

And I've decided to keep my end of the bargain.

Chapter 1

I was sitting in the alcove under the stairs reading *Young Romance* when I heard my mom call me, but I ignored her because I was at the best part of the story. A few minutes later, I heard my sister's footsteps growing louder, thumping on the hardwood floor, making it difficult to concentrate.

Jeannie poked her head into my hiding spot. "C'mon, Lou. Mom said we gotta go."

"Fine." I groaned, rolling up the magazine to bring along.

I dreaded these trips to the old folks' home to see Aunt Violet, but I wasn't allowed to say so since I was only eleven years old. The last time I complained about going, I had my mouth washed out with soap.

We piled into the car, and before we'd even left the driveway, Dad was already talking with Mom about his favorite subject: Communism and Senator McCarthy. I tuned out, preferring to stare out the window and watch the neighborhood go by.

Chicago wasn't very pretty, I decided. It was too plain. Too flat. And the homes all looked the same. When I grew up, I planned to move out west and marry a rancher. I'd have horses and live on acres of land surrounded by mountains. I'd never been out west, but I felt it was my fate.

"You wanna play dolls?" Jeannie asked, interrupting my thoughts.

"I'm reading," I stated while unrolling my magazine.

Jeannie gave me a look that said, "You're not reading. You're looking out the window." I ignored her and buried my nose between the pages. I hated when she bugged me to play dolls. I wasn't a little kid anymore.

Shortly after getting immersed in the story, I heard the crunch of gravel under the tires. I looked up and saw the faded green building, and my heart sank. The place was depressing. Even the exterior looked tired.

On the way in, my mom turned to face me. "Remember what I told you," she said with a stern look.

"I remember." I nodded.

Jeannie grinned at me, and I almost giggled.

On our last visit, I'd made the mistake of asking, "What's that awful smell?" I guess I'd said it loudly too, because everyone in the room looked at me: the nurses, several old men and women, my mother. The look she gave me promised the spanking of all spankings once we got home.

I smiled at Jeannie. At least I could get away with that.

As we walked inside, the familiar stench hit my nostrils, and I cringed. I wondered how everyone could be going about their business acting normal, showing no reaction to the nauseating smell. Once we made it to Aunt Violet's room, Mom opened the door and smiled brightly.

"Hey. Look who's here to see you," she said in a sweet voice.

Everyone smiled and waved on cue. We all lined up to give her a hug and a kiss. When it was my turn, I couldn't decide which was worse, the smell of the old folks' home or her powdery perfume, applied in layers so thick it lingered in my nostrils long after I pulled away, threatening to suffocate me.

While my parents talked to her about how she was feeling, I gazed at the framed photos on the wall. They were pictures of Aunt Violet and her late husband, Irving, through the years. My favorite was the one of Aunt Violet in her blue sequined gown. She was so elegant and beautiful when she was a ballroom dancer.

I glanced at the older woman who sat on the bed, her snow-white hair pinned in place in an attempt at beauty, her skin heavily wrinkled and her hands gnarled. As I stared, she tried to get out of bed and cried out in pain. I jumped at the awful sound.

Mom and Dad rushed to help her while Jeannie and I watched, horrified. Aunt Violet looked frightened and frail. Once she got her footing, Mom helped her shuffle to the restroom.

I looked up at her when she came back into the room on her own. I was certain she would fall. Somehow, she made it back to her bed.

"And how has Miss Louise been lately?" she asked, smiling. "What have you got there?"

I tucked my chin, embarrassed. "A romance comic," I mumbled.

She nodded approval. "I see. Already learning the ways. You're growing up so fast, kiddo. And getting so pretty. I'll bet you'll have so many suitors wanting to marry you they'll have to fight to the death to make you their bride."

I smiled. Aunt Violet had a flair for drama. Mom had said that Aunt Violet used to tell her bedtime stories when she was little, but not the kind you read in a book. Instead, Aunt Violet made them up. Mom had always looked forward to story time.

Aunt Violet turned her attention to Jeannie. "What's your doll's name?" she asked.

Jeannie glanced at me. I nodded toward Aunt Violet. "Tell her," I whispered.

Jeannie turned back to Aunt Violet. "Jane," she said, lifting the doll.

Everyone smiled, and the adults resumed their conversation. I pretended to read, but this time I was eavesdropping. They talked about Aunt Violet's health, and words like rheumatoid arthritis, inflammation levels, and joint destruction filled the small room. I didn't know what any of it meant, but none of it sounded good, and I was thankful when it was time to go.

Later on, after I'd helped with the dinner dishes, I went outside to play. Some of the neighborhood kids were pitching pennies, so I joined them.

"Where have you been?" Bernice asked.

"Old folks' home." She knew better than to ask how it went. I'd already told her how much I disliked going there.

"You wanna play?" she asked, holding up a coin.

"I don't have anything to lose today," I said.

Bernice nodded. She was the best at the game, but instead of collecting the loser's coins, she got paid in candy. She preferred bubble gum, but she'd take marbles, baseball cards, or whatever they'd agreed on beforehand if her opponents didn't have any.

I watched as each of the players took their shot. Frankie's penny got pretty close to the wall, but when Bernice threw hers, it hit the brick surface and dropped straight down.

"Damn it," Frankie cursed. "How do you do it every time?"

Bernice smiled. "Just lucky, I guess."

The first two boys each handed her a piece of gum. Frankie reluctantly gave Bernice one of his marbles, spat on the ground, and walked away.

"He's such a sore loser," I said once we were alone.

Bernice shrugged. "You want some gum?"

"Sure." I took a stick from her, unwrapped it, and popped it in my mouth.

We spent the next half hour practicing pitching pennies. She showed me her technique, claiming it was all in the wrist, but I was never able to master it.

It was still light out but getting late.

"I better get back home and put this away," Bernice said, holding up the marble and winking. She had a wooden box where she stored her winnings. It was so organized the marbles were separated by color in their own compartments.

"Okay. See you tomorrow."

I should have gone home too, but I decided to climb my favorite tree instead. It was the one place where no one could disturb me. It's where I always went when I wanted to be alone.

The sun began to set, so I leaned against a large branch and watched. As the sky turned varying shades of orange and pink, I let myself visit a familiar daydream. Imaginary mountains filled the horizon, and I glanced at them from atop my black horse, Maximilian. We'd just returned from an exhilarating ride, and it was time to put him back in his stall so I could eat dinner with my handsome husband and well-behaved kids.

I heard someone whistle and looked down. There was just enough light left for me to see a colored boy walking down the street by himself.

But he wasn't alone. The whistle had come from one of the older neighborhood boys, who was silently gesturing for his buddies to follow.

"Shit," I said in a half-whisper.

I wanted to head home, but I couldn't climb down because it would attract too much attention. So I waited. When the colored boy turned the corner, the group of white kids took off running after him, so I slid down and dropped to the ground, scraping the palms of my hands on the bark and twisting my ankle in the process.

Shouting erupted in the distance, and I took the opportunity to run away as fast as I could. Fear trumped the pain in my ankle, and I made it home in record time. As I bolted through the front door and slammed it shut behind me, I came face to face with my mom. Her arms were crossed in front of her chest, and she glared at me.

"Do you know what time you're supposed to be home?" she asked, anger bubbling just beneath the surface of her words.

I looked down. "Before dark," I mumbled.

"You're grounded!" she shouted. "Now, get to your room."

I didn't make eye contact. I just ran past her as quickly as I could in the hopes I might avoid a spanking. I made it to my room unscathed, changed into pajamas, and climbed into bed. As I lay there, I wondered what the colored boy was doing walking around all by himself. They had their side of the tracks, and we had ours. And no one ever crossed them.

Chapter 2

The next morning, my mom took my romance comics away and handed me a sponge, Ajax, and a bucket, and told me to clean the bathroom. I had planned to meet Bernice and go bike riding. Instead, I was stuck doing chores.

I scrubbed and scrubbed the clawfoot tub and was surprised to find out just how much elbow grease it took to clean. You'd think all the dirt would just drain away after every bath. An hour later, I had finished the whole bathroom and stood to examine my work. The room sparkled and smelled fresh, filling me with a sense of accomplishment.

My dad came up beside me. "It's spotless. Great job," he said, glancing over his shoulder. He turned back to me. "Here. Take this." He handed me a Fanny May Pixie from the box Mom had just gotten for her birthday.

"Thanks." I smiled, and as I did, he put his finger to his lips to indicate it was our secret. I nodded, then went to my room and enjoyed the delicious treat, a mixture of caramel and nuts drenched in milk chocolate.

I lay on my bed, fully aware it was only a matter of time before my mom gave me another task, which was her special way of driving home the "you will submit to the rules" message. The rules really weren't that difficult to follow. My parents were kind and fair. The problem was me. I was headstrong. Where Jeannie listened and behaved like a model child, I did the opposite, and no amount of punishment seemed to alter my behavior.

Jeannie opened the bedroom door, her doll tucked under her arm.

"What's going on?" I asked.

"Nothing." She came and sat down next to me. "I'm bored."

If I weren't grounded, I would've been outside with my

friends. I didn't know what Jeannie did while I was away and mostly didn't care. But today, I felt a kinship with her. "You want to play a game?" I asked.

Her eyes brightened. "Sure. Which one do you want to play?"

"How about Candy Land?" It was her favorite.

Jeannie smiled and went to get it from the hallway closet. An hour later, I was surprised to realize how much I was enjoying playing with my usually annoying sister. I made a mental note to spend more time with her from now on.

Jeannie belched loudly, and we both started laughing. Mom walked in wearing a serious look, which was quickly replaced by a happy face when she saw us enjoying ourselves. I made eye contact with her, and she suppressed her smile just enough to remind me who's boss.

"Do you want me to clean anything else?" I asked, standing up. I hoped it would make me appear obedient. I wanted her to know she'd won.

"Not right now," she answered. "I'm going to start lunch, and then we're going to the store to shop for school supplies."

When she left, I noticed Jeannie had braided her doll's hair. I looked at Jeannie's unruly mane. "How about I braid your hair to match the doll's?"

Her face lit up. "Okay. Let me grab my brush."

Jeannie rushed from the room, and after she returned, I spent the next half hour removing the tangles and weaving her hair into an intricate ponytail. "There. Now you and Jane match," I said as she inspected the finished result in the mirror.

We sat down to eat egg salad sandwiches, and Mom eyed Jeannie. "Your hair looks pretty."

Jeannie smiled. "Lou did it."

Mom glanced at me, and I grinned. I could tell she didn't want to stay mad at me, but she always tried to keep a serious face for a day or two after I'd disobeyed — like that made the punishment stick better or something. She'd grounded me for a week once before, when I'd slipped up and said the wrong thing at the nursing home, but that was different. She wasn't just angry that time; she was embarrassed. Mortified was the word she'd used.

On the way to the store, we passed Bernice and some of the neighborhood kids. They were having fun playing hopscotch. I wished I could join them and realized if I listened to my parents more often, I wouldn't suffer so much.

"Which notebook do you prefer? Blue or green?" Mom asked as she held up one of each.

"Doesn't matter." I had an opinion on everything I wasn't supposed to have an opinion on, but when asked about topics relevant to my little world, I couldn't care less.

I rounded the corner to look at the comic books while Mom and Jeannie continued shopping. A teenage boy stood reading a magazine. I recognized him as one of the boys I'd seen following the colored kid. When I reached for *Young Romance*, I noticed his eye was black and blue.

He leered at me. "Beat it. I'm reading here," he said.

I put the comic back on the rack and left, irritated he had bossed me around and secretly delighted he'd been smacked in the face. They might have beaten up the colored boy, but it looked like he had gotten at least one good punch in.

I didn't know what all the fuss was about over people's skin color. It seemed silly, and it wasn't like any of us had a choice in the matter. Conveniently, the subject came up at the dinner table that night.

"They're coming to the school this year," Dad said, sounding concerned.

Mom sighed. "Well, there's nothing we can do about it."

"We could send the kids to private school."

"That costs money," Mom said. Dad frowned at that.

I wanted to say I didn't care and not to worry, but I kept my mouth shut. I continued eating my meal in silence while Jeannie played with her food, oblivious to their concerns.

My confinement ended a few days later, and I was allowed to leave the house. Dad had given me a watch so I could keep better track of time, but in my rush to get outdoors, I'd forgotten to put it on.

The hot wind tousled my hair as I rode my bike to the park. I usually wore it in a ponytail so it wouldn't get messy, but today I left it loose, a fitting symbol of my newfound freedom. On my way there, I kept my eyes peeled for Bernice. I didn't see her in any of the usual places, and when I got to the park, she wasn't there either.

Oddly enough, no one was there. I had the place all to myself.

I hopped off my bike and ran to the swing set. After I'd gotten situated in the center swing, I grabbed hold of the heavy chains and pushed off the ground. I pumped my legs to propel myself upwards, and the higher I climbed, the more exhilarated I felt. It was almost as if I could touch the sky. I leaned back and let my legs go limp, gliding back and forth like a human pendulum.

When Mom was around, she wouldn't let me do it. She claimed it was too dangerous, and I could get hurt. But it was my favorite thing to do.

After I'd taken a few more turns, I was ready to leave. I was just about to get on my bike when I saw Bernice. She put her hands on her hips. "Let me guess. You were grounded."

"That would be correct," I replied as I set the bike against the kickstand. I said it without shame, even though I knew it wasn't something to be proud of. There were lots of kids who thought that kind of thing was cool, but Bernice wasn't one of them.

"Well, you missed some neighborhood gossip," she said as she sat on the park bench.

"Yeah? What's that?" I sat beside her.

"Frankie's older brother got into a fight with a colored boy who was walking around here the other night. I guess a group of older kids chased him back to his side of town, but before things ended, there was a fight, and the colored boy clocked him good."

I thought of the boy at the store. Bernice and I had never discussed race, and I wasn't sure how she felt about the situation, so I didn't voice my opinion. With my parents, I was abrupt, often to my own detriment, but I tended to be more careful when I spoke with Bernice.

"I heard they're going to be at school with us this year," I said, giving no hint of my feelings on the matter.

She stared at the other side of the playground. "My mom was talking to my grandma about it on the phone the other night. They don't think it's a good thing."

I raised an eyebrow.

"My family isn't prejudiced or anything," she said. "They just think there will be trouble at school. And you know my parents. It's all about learning with them. They don't want anything to interfere with that."

I thought about my dad's comment, that he'd like to send us to a private school but couldn't because it was too expensive. I was going to tell her about it but decided not to since her family had more money than ours. It wasn't like they were rich. I mean, they lived in our neighborhood and all, but they definitely had more. Bernice told me a story once about her uncle being a successful author, and that he had left them some money when he died.

"Well, let's hope there won't be any trouble then," I said.

Bernice sighed. "If the rumors I've been hearing are true, I don't think hope will make a difference."

Chapter 3

The first week of school, there was tension in the air. Bernice and I took a seat in our classroom as a few colored kids arrived and sat at desks in the back. Mrs. Jenkins looked nervous. Her eyes darted around the room, and as she wrote her name on the chalkboard, she accidentally bumped the eraser with her hip, and it fell to the ground, sending white powder into the air. A couple of boys snickered, and she quickly turned, trying to figure out who had mocked her but couldn't as they'd all become blank-faced.

"Okay. Settle down, everyone. We need to take attendance," she said.

Mrs. Jenkins called our names one by one, and afterward, she asked everyone to write an essay about what they did over the summer.

"Yes?" Mrs. Jenkins said to the new colored girl who had raised her hand.

Everyone stared at the girl.

"I don't have a pencil," she said. "I forgot to bring one."

She made eye contact with me, and I instinctively rose and handed her the extra one I had.

"Thanks," she said.

"No problem," I replied.

I sat back down and caught Frankie glaring at me. Apparently, he had a problem with my not having a problem. I held his gaze and smirked, making it clear I wasn't looking for his approval. Then, I began writing the essay, describing the highs and lows of my summer in vivid detail. Mrs. Jenkins came around and collected it when everyone had finished.

I played tag at recess with Bernice and some other kids. As I ran to tell the other girl, "you're it," I saw the colored girl from our classroom sitting on a swing by herself. She was staring at the ground, looking lonely.

When there was a pause in the game, I ran over to her. "Do you want to play with us?" I asked.

"Okay," she said, smiling brightly. We ran back to the group to start another round.

"Sandy is going to play with us," I said. "Who wants to be it this time?"

My question was greeted with silence. The other kids just glanced at each other and wordlessly walked away. Stunned by their response, I suddenly wished I hadn't invited her. I was just trying to be nice, not make my friends mad at me.

Bernice was the only one who stayed, but she didn't look happy about it.

"I'll be it," Bernice finally said, stepping forward.

I nodded, thankful she'd put herself on the line so I wouldn't look foolish in front of Sandy, who stood next to me, showing no outward sign of how she felt inside.

Bernice shouted, "Go!" and Sandy and I took off running across the empty field. The sound of chirping birds mixed with our laughter made me smile. The sun was blinding and bright, and I soaked it up, enjoying the warmth and the joy of the moment. But when I went to shield my eyes, I noticed a group of kids watching the developing scene with displeasure. A few teachers also looked on with folded arms and some kind of quiet judgment.

On the way home from school, Frankie caught up with me. His plump face was twisted in anger.

"You think you're real smart, don't you?" he said.

I grinned. "Well, my grades are above average. Not straight A's, but—"

"Cut the crap, Lou. You're treading into dangerous territory."

I laughed. "Those are some big words, Frank. Did you read that line in a *Superman* comic? You can read, can't you?"

Frankie pushed me, and the books I was carrying fell into

the street. "I don't have to listen to this shit. You're the one that's going to lose all your friends. Then let's see how smart you are."

I tried to think up a witty comeback as he walked away but couldn't. He left with his head held high as I was forced to gather my things from the dirty pavement. When I had finished collecting them, I noticed a few of the girls in my classroom passing by on their way home. I smiled at them, but they ignored me. Then they began whispering.

My stomach tightened. Maybe Frankie was right.

I felt down during dinner, so after helping with the dishes, I decided to join my sister in the backyard to play, hoping that might cheer me up. She was on a cartwheel kick, but I didn't care for them much, so I stood off to the side, wondering how many she could do before she wiped out. It didn't take long for my sadness to evaporate. Jeannie was really good at cartwheels – and she was having a ton of fun. It was kind of hard not to get caught up in that.

We played hide and seek for a while after that and then came inside and collapsed on the sofa.

"Go get your brush," I told her. "Your hair is a mess." It wasn't that messy, but I knew she liked to fuss over it and figured I'd indulge her. Plus, I enjoyed hanging out with her. She didn't judge me or criticize me like the other kids.

Jeannie grabbed the brush from her room, and we went to the kitchen. She had just taken a seat when Mom turned and said, "Not at the table." So Jeannie and I got up and marched to the bedroom, where I began gently removing the tangles from the bottom before working my way up.

"Are you really gonna get married and move out west?" Jeannie asked out of the blue.

"I hope so," I answered, surprised she had remembered my daydream. I finished smoothing the last of her locks and handed the brush back to her. "Why do you ask?"

She turned to me, looking like she was about to cry.

14

"Because I don't want you to move away. I would miss you."

Her admission tugged at my heart, and I gave her a hug. "Don't worry," I said. "If I move there, you can come visit all the time. I'll be rich, so you'll have your own room, your own horse."

"I like horses," she said in a small voice.

"See. Nothing to be sad about. We'll always be together, no matter what."

Jeannie smiled. And just like that, her worries seemed to be forgotten. Later that night, I lay in bed awake, my mind heavy with concerns of my own. I was haunted by Frankie's comment. I didn't want to become an outcast and lose my friends over Sandy. She meant nothing to me compared to them, but I felt it was unfair I had to choose.

Over the next few months, I distanced myself from Sandy. I was polite to her but didn't invite her to play at recess and didn't show her any extra kindness. This made me feel terrible in those moments when I imagined what it must be like to be in her shoes. Sure, the other kids warmed up to me again, but rejecting Sandy still made me feel bad.

I spent a lot of time hanging out at Bernice's on Christmas break. Her mom had become obsessed with baking pies, and we'd both become willing taste testers.

While enjoying a slice, I said to Bernice, "Tell me more about your uncle who was an author."

She gulped her milk. "You want to know about him or the novel he wrote?"

"Both," I said and took another bite of pie.

Bernice rose and grabbed a book off the shelf. "Here," she said, handing it to me. I read the title: *High Desert Love* by Judith Johnson.

"Wait a minute. I thought you said your uncle wrote this."

"He did. Judith Johnson is a pen name. My mom said he thought the book would sell better if readers thought a woman had written it."

"Huh," I said. "Smart."

I turned it over and read the description: *A sweeping tale of romance amidst the Sangre de Cristo Mountains.* High Desert Love *tells the story of one woman's journey out west and the chance encounter that changes her destiny.*

"This story is set in the west?" I asked, suddenly intrigued. I hadn't told Bernice my dream. Only my sister knew.

"Yeah. My uncle lived in Santa Fe, New Mexico, so that's where he set the novel."

I held the book in my hand. I was dying to read it even though it was for grown-ups. "Did you ever meet him?" I asked.

"Once, when I was little, but I don't remember much about him other than he reeked of alcohol."

"Oh," I replied. "I thought he might've had a more interesting story."

Bernice's mom came into the room and took our plates. "He's got an interesting story, all right," she joked. "Your aunt's the best one to tell it."

I eyed Bernice. "Your aunt?" She'd never mentioned her aunt.

"Yeah. I'm going to visit her next summer."

"In Santa Fe?"

"Yep. She's got a ranch out there, and she invited me to stay for a few weeks."

I was instantly jealous.

"Why don't you come with me?" Bernice suggested. "It would be so much fun."

I tsked. "My parents would never let that happen."

"You never know," Bernice said. "Try kissing up to them for a few months. They might say yes."

Chapter 4

Mom, Dad, Jeannie, and I rang in the New Year with Guy Lombardo and his big band, enjoying it for the first time on TV. Mom had put out a tray of appetizers, which we nibbled on while watching the show and sipping our drinks – champagne flutes for them and apple juice in fancy cups for Jeannie and me. When a song Mom and Dad really liked came on, they started dancing. Jeannie and I attempted to dance too, but we didn't know the right steps, so we just ended up shimmying and giggling while making silly faces at each other.

The next day brought the new and improved me. The me who would do whatever it took to schmooze my parents into letting me go with Bernice to Santa Fe next summer. Mom complained of a headache in the morning, so I offered to do the dishes after breakfast so she could rest. At dinnertime, I set the table, and I could feel her studying me, probably trying to figure out what was going on. I thought she might say something, but she didn't. She just continued watching me without comment.

Three weeks later, after I'd done a myriad of chores without being asked, turned in all my homework, and had come home on time every day, I was sure I'd made inroads into my parents' good graces. The time seemed right to launch into my travel campaign.

Mom and Dad were sitting on the sofa discussing Aunt Violet while Jeannie played with her doll nearby, so I joined them, pretending to be interested in their conversation. When they had finished talking, I glanced at my mom and casually said, "Did you know Bernice's uncle wrote a romance novel?"

Mom looked intrigued. "No. I didn't." She held my gaze, waiting for me to say more, but as she stared, it felt like her eyes were boring holes into my skull, like she already knew my master plan.

"Yeah. Bernice said he wrote it under a pen name, so people would think he was a woman," I added.

"Weird," Jeannie blurted.

I shot her a look that said "Zip it," then turned back to Mom and smiled. "The book is called *High Desert Love*. It's set in Santa Fe, New Mexico, where he used to live."

My words sounded stilted, like I was reading a prepared speech. My hands felt clammy as I eyed my mom, hoping she couldn't tell how nervous I was.

"Used to live?" Dad asked, helping me without knowing it.

"Yeah. He died, but Bernice's aunt still lives there. She's got a big ranch with horses, and she invited Bernice to come visit her for a few weeks next summer. She said I was welcome to come, too," I mentioned like it was no big deal.

Mom and Dad glanced at each other. I could see I'd thrown them a curveball. Jeannie's eyes grew wide as she realized the importance of what I had just said, but I nodded at her ever so slightly, warning her to keep quiet.

"Well, that was very nice of Bernice's aunt to offer, but we couldn't afford to send you there," Mom said.

I'd already anticipated her response and was ready with a reply. "It's not going to cost anything because Bernice and her parents are driving there. I'd just be an extra person in the car."

Mom mulled over the idea, her expression unsure. "But we don't know Bernice's aunt. We've never even met her, and you'll only be twelve this summer."

I turned to Dad. "We'll think about it," he said, raising his eyebrows, which meant we were done talking about it for now.

At dinner, I was quiet, my mind busy working on trying to find a new angle that would get them to let me go, but I was out of ideas. So I went to my room and pouted afterward, certain my life was ruined.

I told Bernice all about it the next day. "Don't worry," she said. "They may still let you go. Just stay on your best behavior."

Being good was exhausting. But it was worth a shot.

For the next few months I was a model child. It went against my nature, but I pretended I was playing a part in a movie. Dad told me Mom was warming up to the trip idea, especially since he had mentioned it would be a great experience for me to have as a child. The only thing she was against was me being in another state with a stranger.

"Your mom could talk to my aunt," Bernice said when I told her the latest. "Just let me know, and I'll mention it to my mom."

I nodded, planning on running it by my dad when I got home. I glanced at the book in her hand.

"Why do you want to learn Spanish?" I asked. We already had enough homework.

"Because in New Mexico half the people are Hispanic and speak Spanish. And my parents thought it would be fun to be able to communicate in both languages."

It sounded to me like her parents were tricking her into doing more work. But Bernice seemed interested, so I was interested, too.

"*Hola. Como estas?*" I repeated after Bernice had said it. We didn't know if we were saying it right.

"*Bien. Y usted?*" We both said multiple times. Then we practiced the lines on each other.

Bernice's mom checked in on us.

"Boy. You two sound good," she complimented. "Keep it up."

After she left, I asked, "Does your mom speak Spanish?"

"No."

"Then how does she know we sound good?"

"She doesn't. She's just saying that because she's happy we're learning."

I thought her mom was odd, but she baked yummy pies and cookies, so I didn't fault her for being a little weird.

"How do you say horse in Spanish?" I asked Bernice when we were finished with the lesson.

She grabbed the Spanish/English dictionary and looked it up. *"El caballo."*

It sounded nice. Later, as I rode my bike home, I repeated it over and over in my head. I burst through the front door and shouted, *"El caballo!"*

Dad lowered his paper and eyed me. "What's that?"

"It's Spanish for horse."

"That's nice, dear," he replied. He lifted his paper and continued reading, oblivious to my dream of living out west, riding into the sunset with Maximilian. But why would he act any differently? I'd never told him my dream. I'd only told Jeannie.

That's when the light bulb went on.

When Mom came to tuck me in that night, I sat up straight and said, "You know how I want to go with Bernice to New Mexico this summer?"

She sighed. "Yes."

"Well, I never told you why it's so important to me."

Mom raised an eyebrow. "Tell me why you think it's so important."

"Because it's my destiny," I said. "Ever since I was little, I've dreamt of moving out west. I want to live on a ranch and have a black horse named Maximilian."

Mom giggled. "Wherever did you get such an idea?" she asked, shaking her head.

"I don't know. I just know it's my fate."

Mom's expression turned serious. "Well, that may be true, honey. You may move out west and live on a ranch when you grow up, but I don't see how it has anything to do with going on the trip with Bernice."

"Don't you see," I said, locking eyes with her. "This is how it starts. Think about it. I've never met anyone who lives out west, yet I know I'll end up there. And now Bernice happens to have an aunt who lives on a ranch out west, and she invites both of us to visit."

She still looked unconvinced.

"Don't you see, if I don't go on this trip, there's a chance my whole life could be thrown off course."

Mom was quiet for a moment before she took a deep breath. "I know it seems like some kind of omen that you've been invited to Bernice's aunt's house, but you're just too young to go. It would be different if your dad and I were going too, but we're not. We don't know Bernice's aunt. We barely know Bernice's parents."

My heart sank. She reached for my face, using her fingers to lift my chin. "I'm not saying Bernice's aunt isn't a nice lady. I'm sure she's wonderful, and it was kind of her to invite you, but I can't allow you to go on a trip across the country. Not this time."

My world was being crushed.

I started crying. Mom frowned, like she felt my pain and cared, then reached for me and gave me a hug.

"Don't get so upset," she said while rubbing my back. "I'm sure Bernice's aunt will invite you again. When you're older."

When she left I lay down and continued sobbing. What if there never was a next time? What if this was my only chance and I was missing it? I resented living in a world where I was told what to do and vowed never to do that to my own children.

Chapter 5

I sulked for days, and Jeannie was the only one at home who seemed to care. As I sat cross-legged on my bedroom floor reading a book, she poked her head in.

"I just did my hair," she said, turning from side to side. "You want me to do yours?"

I managed to smile. "Sure."

She came in and took a seat on the bed behind me, brush in hand, and began going through the tangles and smoothing them, working from left to right. She hummed as she braided, which put me at ease and lifted my spirits ever so slightly. When she had finished, she turned to me and said, "You wanna go outside and play? We could climb a tree."

Jeannie was afraid of heights, but she knew how much I liked climbing trees. Her kindness almost made me want to cry.

I was about to say maybe another time because I was tired, when Mom called out from the kitchen: "I made brownies."

I had been on a hunger strike ever since she ruined my life, but brownies were my very favorite food. I knew exactly what she was up to, and I wanted to stand my ground, but Jeannie wore an excited expression.

"Brownies! C'mon," she said.

Reluctantly, I followed her to the kitchen and took a seat. Mom set the plate of brownies in the center of the table and poured us each a glass of milk. I took a bite of one, which was delicious and melted in my mouth, but tried not to let the satisfaction show on my face.

"I've got a fun day planned for us," she announced. "There's a carnival nearby, and we're taking you there this afternoon. They have games, rides. They even have a carousel with horses," she said, eyeing me and smiling.

"All right!" Jeannie exclaimed, practically jumping out of her chair.

I put the rest of my brownie down and pushed the plate away. I didn't want to go to a stupid carnival.

Mom ignored my reaction. "Okay. We'll head out as soon as you're both ready," she said.

Jeannie raced down the hallway to wash her hands. I went to my room and stared in the mirror, feeling sorry for myself. No wooden horse could ever compare with Maximilian.

After I had changed, I shuffled to the family room, where Jeannie, Mom, and Dad were waiting.

"Who's ready to have a great time?" Dad asked.

"I am," I answered flatly.

Dad looked disappointed by my lackluster response, but he put on a big smile and said, "Let's get going then."

The carnival was packed. Amusement park music filled the air, along with peals of laughter as kids of all ages ran to and fro with pink and blue clouds of cotton candy. Even though we'd just had brownies, Jeannie wanted cotton candy, too. And since Dad was going out of his way to make us happy, he said yes.

After sharing a pink cloud of sticky sugar, Jeannie and I ran around checking out all the rides. On my way past the Tilt-A-Whirl, I spotted Frankie. He was waiting in line with one of his friends and was just about to board. He saw me and waved, so I waved back. He'd been a bit nicer since I'd backed away from Sandy, but I still didn't care for him. He was a bully.

I watched him climb into the cart and sit next to his buddy. His round face and puffy cheeks made him look like a pig, and I smirked as I thought of the Spanish word for pig: *puerco*. I could call him that to his face and he wouldn't have a clue what it meant. As the ride started and he and his friend began spinning, I smiled, the secret knowledge filling me with a sense of satisfaction.

"Which one do you want to go on?" Jeannie asked. She looked eager.

"I don't care. You pick."

Jeannie spied the screaming kids on the Tilt-A-Whirl. "How about that one?"

I wasn't sure if I would like it, but we got in line. Our parents caught up to us, and Jeannie asked, "Are you coming, too?"

"We'll watch you from here," Dad said. Something about his expression told me spinning rides weren't his thing. I glanced at Mom. She gazed at me, wearing a hopeful expression, but I turned away and started chatting with Jeannie.

When Frankie got off the ride, he looked ill. His pale freckled skin was tinged yellowish-green, and he swayed as he walked. Jeannie and I were next, so we climbed the stairs and hopped in an open cart. Once they were all filled, the ride began. It started off slowly, and I was about to say "this isn't so bad" when it quickly accelerated, spinning out of control. The crowd blurred as I screamed and slid into Jeannie, the pressure so strong I worried I might crush her. Unharmed, she threw her hands in the air and howled at the tops of her lungs with delight.

I stumbled as I got off, and Jeannie grabbed my arm.

"You okay?" she asked.

"Just a little dizzy," I said.

Jeannie grinned. "I loved it. I could go again."

Mom and Dad approached. "How about we go on the carousel next," Dad suggested.

I had no interest in wooden horses, but I figured I'd get it over with. At least it would make my parents happy.

We boarded and I searched for a black horse. I didn't see one, so I chose a white one instead. The saddle was decorated with pink and purple jewels and the reins were painted gold. And soon I was moving up and down, riding in a circle to nowhere.

Mom sat on the horse just ahead of me on the left. Halfway through the ride, she turned back to see if I was having a good time, but I didn't make eye contact. I just continued staring into the space ahead, thinking how pointless this idea was.

I fell asleep on the car ride home. The sugar buzz had worn off, and so had the adrenalin rush from one last visit to the Tilt-A-Whirl to satisfy Jeannie's need for speed. I woke much later in my bed, confused where I was for a moment. Wide awake, I reached for the flashlight I kept under my bed and began reading one of my romance comics, preferring the fiction of the story to the reality of my crummy life.

At the end of the school year, my parents hadn't budged on their decision. Bernice knew I felt awful but told me to keep my chin up, and promised we'd do it again when we were a little older. "It will be even more fun then because I'll know my way around."

"I guess," I mumbled.

I couldn't believe I had wasted all that effort on being good. It hadn't gotten me anywhere.

"You want to go to a movie before I leave?" Bernice asked.

"Sure," I replied.

As we walked to the theater, I kept thinking about how Bernice was embarking on an adventurous journey while I was left to climb the same old trees and take trips to the nursing home to see Aunt Violet.

Once we got to the cinema, I noticed a John Wayne movie was playing, which piqued my interest.

"How about *The Searchers*?" I suggested.

"Sounds good," Bernice said.

The bored ticket attendant took our money without even asking our ages; Bernice treated us to popcorn, and we took a seat. Cartoons played before the movie, and when the film finally started, everybody quieted down.

I was captured by the setting as much as the story. The main character, Ethan, had returned to Texas after fighting in the Civil War, and when his niece Debbie was abducted, he set out to find her. His journey took him to New Mexico, of all places, and I found myself smiling despite his sorrow as I watched the beautiful scenery.

Someday it would be my turn.

On the way home, I turned to Bernice. "I have a secret I never told you."

"Really? What is it?" she asked, slowing her pace.

I wasn't sure why I hadn't told her before, but it seemed like the right time. As we walked home, I told her of my dream to live out west. I divulged every detail.

"I know it's my fate," I said. "I'm certain of it."

Bernice held up her arm. "Look," she said. "I've got chills."

Sure enough, she had goose bumps.

"What do you think?" I asked.

"I think it's a shame you're not coming this summer. I think it's more than a shame. I think it's detrimental."

I studied her. I wasn't sure what detrimental meant, but I figured it was serious.

"I don't think it's a coincidence that this opportunity showed up when it did," Bernice said.

"I know exactly what you mean," I said. "I tried to explain it to my mom, but she doesn't get it."

"Maybe she does get it. Maybe she's just thinking about your age. Isn't that what she keeps saying? That you're too young?"

She had a point. Maybe my mom wasn't stupid after all. Maybe she was only seeing one side. But since she was the one who had the final say, her side was the only one that mattered.

When we got to Bernice's house, her mom was making dinner, so I didn't stay long. I gave Bernice a hug.

"Have fun," I said. I started to leave, but she told me to wait a minute, disappeared into the other room, then reappeared with her mom, who was holding a book.

"Why don't you borrow this," Bernice's mom said.

I took it from her and smiled. It was *High Desert Love* by Judith Johnson.

Chapter 6

With Bernice gone, I hung out with the other neighborhood kids. Some of them were fun and enjoyed playing the games I liked, but a lot of times they just wanted to stand around and talk about stupid stuff, like the black family that had just moved to our side of town.

"My dad says they all came to Chicago from the South looking for jobs."

"Well, they've got a lot of nerve moving here," another said angrily.

As they gossiped, I stayed busy practicing cartwheels. I wished we could play tag or pitch pennies. I couldn't wait until Bernice came home. These kids were kind of boring.

"What do you think?" one of them asked me.

"About what?" I answered, pretending I hadn't been following their conversation.

"About the niggers that just moved in near your house?"

I couldn't tell them my true feelings, that it didn't bother me. That would just create more problems than I'd had with Sandy.

"I don't know," I answered. "I haven't really given it much thought."

The older boy, Kevin, didn't buy my response. "Whatever," he grunted.

I shrugged and checked my watch. "Shoot. I'm supposed to be home already. We're having company. See you guys." I waved goodbye.

"Later," one of them mumbled.

On my way home, I decided to make myself scarce until Bernice returned. She would only be gone three more weeks, and I'd rather hang out with my younger sister than with the boring neighborhood kids. Besides, I had a novel to finish.

The next day, I was immersed in chapter four when Jeannie came into my room.

"Why are you so dressed up?" I asked.

"We're going to Aunt Violet's today. It's her 80th birthday."

I had forgotten all about that. I quickly searched for a nice dress of my own and ended up choosing a pink floral one that was hanging at the end of the closet. I couldn't remember when I wore it last, and when I changed into it, I noticed the shoulders were snug.

Mom came into the room, looking frantic. "We're running late," she said. "Are you ready?"

"Almost. I just have to change my shoes."

I slipped on a nicer pair, and we were off. As we got closer to our destination, a familiar dread set in. Aunt Violet had always been kind to me, and my mom really liked her, so where the feelings came from was a mystery.

On the way there, we went through the usual routine where Mom told me to behave and not say anything that would embarrass her, and I nodded, realizing I'd never live that episode down. She told me to carry Aunt Violet's present while she held the flowers, and as we entered the building, a nurse wearing a wide smile greeted us.

"Isn't that nice," she commented. She winked at me, and I felt even guiltier for not wanting to be there.

"Happy Birthday!" Mom said as we walked into Aunt Violet's room.

The older woman smiled, and I could see a twinkle in her eye even though she was lying in bed. "Thank you, dear," she said.

Mom put the flowers next to her bed, and I handed her the present.

"Happy Birthday," I repeated. Jeannie chimed in a few seconds after me.

"Now, don't I feel special," Aunt Violet said. "Three beautiful girls got all gussied up and came to see an old lady when they could've been doing something much more exciting."

"What could be more exciting than spending time with you?" Mom replied.

I thought Aunt Violet was pretty boring but figured she must have been more fun when she was young because Mom often talked about all the good times they had together.

Aunt Violet began unwrapping her gift, and I was surprised to see it was a romance novel.

"I've been wanting this one. Thank you," she said, acknowledging all of us.

"My friend's uncle wrote a romance novel," I said.

Aunt Violet looked impressed. "Really? What's it called?"

"*High Desert Love* by Judith Johnson. He wrote it under a pen name," I added after seeing her puzzled expression.

"Can't say I've heard of it. I'll have to add it to my reading list."

I swelled with pride even though he wasn't my uncle.

Mom spent some time talking to Aunt Violet about how she was feeling, and from what I could tell, it didn't sound good. This confused me because Aunt Violet looked so happy all the time, at least whenever we were around.

When we got back home, Jeannie and I ran outside to play. I practiced tricks with my Yo-Yo, deep in thought.

"I don't want to get old," I said.

"How come?" Jeannie asked.

"Because Aunt Violet looks like she's just sitting there waiting to die. I don't want to be like that. I say eighty and out."

Jeannie looked confused. "You mean you don't want to live past eighty?"

"Exactly."

"But what if you don't die before then?"

I caught my Yo-Yo and turned to face her, running my index finger across my neck while making a slicing sound.

Jeannie laughed. "You're funny."

I didn't smile.

"But you're kidding, right?"

"Nope."

I had never been surer of anything in my life. I knew it like I knew I'd live out west and feed carrots to Maximilian. "What do you say? You in?"

Jeannie put her hands on her hips and scrunched her face as she thought about it. "I'm in," she said, reaching for my hand.

We shook on it, and with that settled, turned our attention to more important things, like the sound of the approaching ice cream truck. We bolted for the front door, and as we came running in, Dad was already standing, pulling money from his pocket.

"Thanks!" we said in unison as we raced toward the truck.

We waited patiently as the other kids took their turns. Jeannie and I both got Good Humor bars, smiling at each other and nodding appreciatively as we devoured our ice cream.

This was living, I thought.

Later that night, I couldn't sleep, so I grabbed my flashlight and pulled *High Desert Love* out of its top-secret hiding spot. I was honored Bernice's mom had lent it to me but didn't think my mom would appreciate me reading a grown-up love story.

I was completely immersed in the plot when I heard a loud explosion outside. I jumped from the bed and peered out the window, and saw a house on fire a few doors down. The colored family's home.

Moments later, a black man and woman came running out in their pajamas. The lady was coughing, unable to stand on her own, so the man held her up as they hurried away from the burning building.

Dad opened my bedroom door. "Get away from the window," he said. Before I could see what happened next, he scooped me in his arms and carried me to the family room, where Mom and a bleary-eyed Jeannie were seated on the sofa.

"What was that loud noise?" I asked, my heart still racing.

Mom glanced at Dad.

"I think it was a Molotov cocktail," Dad said.

"What's that?" I asked.

"It's a bomb," Dad answered, taking a seat next to me.

"Aren't we supposed to duck and cover?" I asked.

"Not this time," Dad said. "It's not like that."

"What do you mean?" I asked.

"Because the bomb was meant for our neighbors."

He and I made eye contact, and then I understood. "You mean someone tried to kill our neighbors?"

"It appears so," Mom said.

"Why would someone do that?" I asked, suddenly feeling frightened.

Mom frowned. "I don't know, honey."

Jeannie started crying, which made me cry.

"Shouldn't we go out there? Shouldn't we see if they need help?" I asked.

I rose, thinking we were all going to race outside, but my parents stayed seated.

"I don't think that's a good idea," Dad cautioned. "It's best not to get involved."

Chapter 7

I was about to head outside the following day when my dad stopped me. "You'll have to play indoors today."

"How come?"

"Because I don't know what's going on yet. I want to make sure it's safe."

He took the trash to the curb while I watched from the window. He talked to the old man across the street, and the man nodded and pointed toward the neighbor's house. I craned my neck to try and see it, but a tree blocked my view. I hurried to my bedroom and looked out that window instead. All that was left of the neighbor's house were a few charred remains.

The front door opened, and I rushed back to find out what Dad had learned. Mom was waiting too, looking just as interested.

"The fire trucks didn't come until it was too late. The house is destroyed." He exchanged a look with Mom.

"Any word on Mr. and Mrs. Williams?" Mom asked.

"No. No one's seen them."

"I saw them escape in their pajamas," I said. "They have to be around somewhere." I turned to my dad. "Where do you think they are?"

"I honestly don't know," he answered.

Since Jeannie and I had to stay inside for the rest of the day, I spent a large part of it thinking about the old neighbors — Mom had referred to them as the Williams family. I hadn't known their name until then. I hoped they were doing okay. Maybe they were staying with friends or relatives. But why would anyone throw a bomb at their house? Who could be so mean? The whole situation made me feel confused and angry.

A week passed, and there was still no news about the Williams family. Life just went on as if nothing had happened.

As if their absence was insignificant. I wished I could forget them too, but I couldn't. I simply had to find out where they were.

Bernice came over the same day she returned home from New Mexico. When I told her about the fire, she was intrigued. "How could they just vanish into thin air?" she asked.

I nodded. "That's what I've been thinking."

"C'mon," she said. "Let's go to my house. Maybe my mom knows something."

I grabbed her uncle's book before we left, and when we walked in, Bernice's mom greeted me with a big smile.

"Louise, long time no see," she said.

I lifted up the novel. "I've been busy reading. Thanks for lending it to me." I handed it to her.

She looked like she was about to say something, but Bernice cut her off. "Hey, Mom, did you hear anything about a fire over by Lou's house?"

Her cheerful expression quickly vanished. "Yes," she said. "The colored family's home."

"Lou says she saw what happened, or at least saw the husband and wife run out of the house, but no one seems to know what happened to them afterward."

Bernice's mom reached for her pack of cigarettes, took one out, and lit it. After she took a puff, she sat on the sofa and stared off into the distance. Bernice and I sat down opposite her, waiting.

"Someone set their house on fire to send them a message," she said, finally. "Someone wanted them to go back to where they came from."

"Really? Where'd you hear that?" Bernice asked.

"A friend of a friend." Bernice's mom was being intentionally vague. It was obvious she didn't trust us enough to spill the details. Still, she had shared more than my parents, assuming they even knew any of this information. "I guess the husband is an editor at *The Chicago Daily Defender*. A newspaper for blacks," she added after taking another drag off her cigarette. "Some people didn't like what they were writing about and wanted to make an example of them."

"Holy shit!" Bernice exclaimed.

"Bernice! Watch your mouth!" her mom scolded.

Bernice's eyes widened, realizing her error. "Sorry," she mumbled.

Bernice had an unusual relationship with her mom, who often treated her as an adult, except when she acted too grown up and had to be put in her place.

"But does anyone know what happened to them?" I asked, trying to take the focus off Bernice's blunder.

"I'm assuming they moved away, but I don't know for sure." She put out her cigarette in the ashtray, then stood up. "Your father will be home soon. I better get dinner started," she said, walking away.

Once she was gone, Bernice shook her head and laughed. "I can't believe I just swore in front of my mother."

"You're lucky I was here or you'd be in deep shit."

Bernice smirked. "So tell me about your vacation," I said. There was no point dwelling on the negative when there were other things to discuss.

"It was a blast. My aunt took us hiking, horseback riding. Oh, and she bought me this bracelet." She thrust her arm out so I could see it. "It's sterling silver with turquoise. Made by Navajo Indians."

It looked more like a cuff than a bracelet, but it was beautiful, with teardrop-shaped turquoise stones that fanned out in a circle, like the sun.

"It's pretty," I said. "I've never seen anything like it."

Bernice smiled. "I know. I love it so much I've worn it every day."

"You said your aunt took *us* hiking. Who's us?"

"Me and my aunt's neighbor, Juan. He's the son of the Mexican family that owns the ranch next door. They're a large family, but Juan's my age, so at least I had someone to hang out with." Bernice wore a dopey smile.

"What are you smiling about?" I asked.

"He's got an older brother, Alejandro." She swooned. "He's the most."

"Oh my God. You like someone. I can't believe it. Does he like you?"

She frowned. "No. He doesn't know I exist."

"I find that hard to believe. Look at you. You're smart. You're beautiful. How could he not notice?"

"Because I'm a kid." She pouted.

"How old is he?"

"Sixteen." She sat up straight and folded her arms across her chest. "The whole time, he was off with his friends, doing his own thing. I tried to get him to come with us a few times, but I guess he didn't want to spend time with a twelve-year-old girl."

Bernice looked sad. I didn't like seeing her that way. "But you had fun hanging out with Juan, right?"

"Sure. He's nice. Like the brother I never had, but I wanted to be near Alejandro."

It was strange hearing Bernice talk about a boy. She had always been focused on school. Now she sounded like a normal person, albeit a heartbroken one.

"Maybe you'll get to see him again. When we go back," I said.

Her shoulders relaxed. "You're right. There's always next time. And Juan is dying to meet you, too."

"Me? Why?"

"Cause you're my best friend, and I told him all about you. He thinks you're cool."

Me, cool? I liked the sound of that. "What do you think Juan's doing right now?" I asked.

"Probably hiking or horseback riding. Or taking a nap."

I wished I could do those kinds of things on my summer breaks.

I was feeling a little sleepy myself now that I thought of it. "Speaking of naps…" I yawned.

"Good idea." Bernice tossed me a throw pillow, and I got comfy on the chair while she stretched out on the sofa. After we closed our eyes, she said, "I told Juan all about Chicago. He hopes to come here someday, too."

"Why would he want to come here?"

"Because he's never been to a big city before. And even though we think it's dull, he thinks it's exciting."

I smiled as I drifted off to sleep, thinking about how most people thought where everyone else lived was better.

Chapter 8

Years passed, and Juan never made it to Chicago to visit Bernice, and sadly, I never got to go to New Mexico. That one summer was Bernice's only trip out west, and I missed the opportunity because I was too young. Her aunt had been ill the following year, and it wasn't a good time. The year after that, there was some other reason. And anyway, now her parents were saving money for her to go to college.

I took a sip of my chocolate malt and tapped my fingers on the table as the jukebox began playing Chubby Checker's *The Twist*.

"Why do you want to go to college?" I asked Bernice. A girl getting an advanced education was unheard of. Then again, Bernice was unique.

"Because my parents think I have a mind for business," she replied, dipping her french fry into a pool of ketchup.

If anyone had a mind for business, it was Bernice. She'd recently started babysitting on the weekends and had been saving eighty percent of her earnings. I had asked her why "eighty percent," and she said it was because she needed to amass as much as she could for school but wanted a little left over for fun.

All I wanted was to get married and have kids. I didn't want to run a business but could see Bernice doing so.

"Which college are you going to?" I asked, hoping it wasn't far away.

"Whichever one I can get into. Not every school lets women attend." She took a sip of her soda and added, "My parents are looking into it."

When we finished eating, Bernice had to run. Her mom had broken her arm, so she was needed at home to help with chores. I was about to leave, too, when I overheard a conversation at the table behind me.

"Call her and ask her on a date," a boy suggested.

"I don't want to go out with her. She's black," another boy replied.

"It's a joke," a familiar voice added. "You're not really going to take her out, just make her think you will and blow her off."

They all laughed, like their idiotic idea was pure genius. I got up and turned to face them.

Frankie was sitting with a group of friends, one of whom I didn't recognize.

"Do you guys have nothing better to do with your time than play childish games?" I asked.

"It's just Sandy," Frankie said. "Give it a rest, Lou."

I'd grown tired of his continued mistreatment of Sandy and was disappointed in myself for not standing up for her more through the years. She and I could have been great friends if I hadn't caved to peer pressure.

I pursed my lips. "I happen to think Sandy is a beautiful girl, and that you'd be *lucky* to get a date with her, considering your appearance."

Frankie had gotten heavier, and my comment must've hit him where it hurt because he stood up, seething with anger.

"Why don't you buzz off? We weren't talking to you anyway."

The boy I didn't know rose. I hadn't paid him any attention at first because I was laser-focused on Frankie. He was attractive, with slicked-back brown hair and green eyes.

"Whoa," he said. "How about we all calm down. Maybe the lady has a point."

The expression on Frankie's face was priceless. He looked like he'd just been slapped.

I smiled, and the boy stepped toward me.

"We were just messing around. We had no intention of calling your friend. Like you said, we've got better things to do."

Defeated, Frankie tossed his napkin on the table and walked

away. The boy kept his eyes locked on me.

"My name's Jim," he said. "And you are?"

"Louise," I answered, softening my tone.

The remaining boys got up and wordlessly headed to the jukebox.

"Nice to meet you, Louise." He looked shy all of a sudden, then sat back down in the booth. I had been planning on leaving but instead sat opposite him.

"I just moved here from New York. Trying to make friends can be a challenge," he said.

I nodded. "Well, most of those guys are decent. It's just Frankie. He's been a jerk for as long as I can remember. He even pushed me down once."

Jim's jaw tensed. "A man should never hit a woman. How dare he?"

His reaction both surprised and comforted me. "We were just kids," I added, trying to downplay the incident.

No guy had ever called me a lady or referred to me as a woman before. It made me feel so grown up.

"That's no excuse," he said, leaning back. "Do you like movies?"

I smiled. "Of course."

"Do you want to go to a movie with me this weekend?"

I gave him an apprehensive look. Not because I didn't want to go, but because I didn't know if my parents would let me.

"It would be nice to spend time with someone who is the kind of friend I'm looking to make," he said, looking so innocent it bordered on angelic.

"I'd have to ask my parents. If you're going to be around here the same time tomorrow, I'll let you know."

Jim checked his watch. "I'll be here."

I got up to leave. "See you tomorrow, then. Nice meeting you."

He rose and smiled. "The pleasure is all mine," he said in a velvety voice.

On my way home, I grinned from ear to ear. Not only was the new boy cute, he made me feel special. And he put Frankie in his place, too.

When I walked in the door, anxious to tell Jeannie all about him, my face fell. Mom was on the sofa crying, and Dad had his arms around her, rubbing her back.

"What's going on?" I asked.

Mom looked up, her face puffy, her eyes red. "Aunt Violet died," she sobbed, falling back into Dad's arms.

I'd never seen my mom cry like that before. I wanted to hug her, to say the right words that would make her feel better, but instead, I ran to my room.

Dad came in a little later. He looked drained. "You okay?" he asked in a soft voice as he sat next to me.

"I guess," I replied. I wondered why I wasn't sad over Aunt Violet's death. We had been visiting her twice a month for years. Shouldn't I be crying? What was wrong with me?

"Aunt Violet lived a long life," he said, interrupting my thoughts. "She was in a lot of pain, but she's in a better place now."

I nodded because he sounded like he knew what he was talking about. "I've never seen Mom so upset. She really loved her, huh?"

"More than you know." Dad let out a deep sigh. "Violet was more like a mother to your mom than her own mother."

"Really?"

"Yes. She was there for her a lot as a kid, through good times and bad, and as an adult, well, let's just say Violet helped us out when we were in a jam once."

I hadn't realized Aunt Violet meant so much to my mom. I thought she just visited her to be nice or out of obligation. Mom had told me about some of the good times they shared, but she never admitted that she was closer to her than her own mom.

The thought of Mom hurting finally brought the stubborn

tears. Dad gave me a hug. He didn't say anything, just held me. When I stopped crying, he gave me a kiss on the forehead.

"Your mom said she'd like to be alone tonight, so she's going to sleep on the sofa. I'm going to bed early. I'm pooped," he admitted.

"Good night," I said. I was exhausted, too, and hadn't even gone to check on Jeannie to see how she was doing. I guessed Dad had already seen her first and tucked her in before checking on me. It was the kind of night where everyone was hitting the hay early.

As I kicked off my shoes, my thoughts turned to Jim. He was really cute, and I liked how he talked to me. I smiled, remembering our conversation, then immediately felt guilty that I was thinking about a boy when a family member had just died. It seemed selfish and wrong.

I lay down, remembering how I used to dread visiting Aunt Violet. It had gotten better once I was older, and we could talk about romance novels, but I always felt uncomfortable there.

My last thought before falling asleep was of the framed photograph hanging on the wall at the nursing home, the one with Aunt Violet wearing a blue sequined gown, looking like a movie star.

I decided that's how I'd always remember her.

I woke in the middle of the night drenched in sweat from a recurring dream. I was at the neighbor's house, trying to help Mr. and Mrs. Williams as flames licked at me from all angles. I searched the rooms one by one, but they were all empty. Realizing they had left, I tried to escape but couldn't because the roof began collapsing on me.

I sat up and tried to catch my breath while wiping my forehead with the back of my hand. I never found out what happened to the neighbors that disappeared and rarely thought of them anymore.

Too bad they wouldn't leave my dreams.

Chapter 9

Early the next morning, I found my mom curled in a fetal position on the couch. She was still asleep, wearing her clothes from the day before, and there were crumpled tissues strewn all over the coffee table.

I tiptoed across the carpet and pulled the quilt over her shoulders, then gathered the tissues off the table and carried them to the kitchen garbage. After I threw them away, I heard the floor creak behind me.

"Hey," Jeannie whispered, still in her pajamas. "You hungry?"

"Yeah." We'd gone to bed without a real dinner. The news of Aunt Violet's passing had left everyone without an appetite. "How about we make breakfast?" I suggested.

Jeannie nodded, then we quietly pulled everything out and began cooking. The aroma of fresh coffee and sizzling bacon wafted through the air, and soon after, Mom came in.

"What's all this?" she asked. She looked like she'd aged several years overnight.

"We thought you could use some help," Jeannie said, which brought the first smile I'd seen on Mom's face since the bad news came.

"Thanks," Mom said. "I really appreciate this."

She set the table while Jeannie and I served the food. Dad came in and took a seat. After taking a bite of his eggs, he said, "Who knew my daughters were such amazing cooks?"

Jeannie and I smiled at the compliment, and we dug into our meal, which did taste pretty darn good.

"We'll have to go to the nursing home today. Take care of things there and make funeral arrangements," Mom said in a quiet voice.

Dad took hold of her hand and squeezed it. "We'll get it all taken care of today," he said.

When we had finished eating, we got cleaned up and drove to the funeral home. Mom and Dad spoke with the man in charge while Jeannie and I waited outside.

"This place gives me the creeps," I said.

"Tell me about it," Jeannie agreed. "It's spooky."

"Poor Aunt Violet. She lived a long life, though. Eighty-four-years-old."

"Too long. The last few years, all she did was lie in bed in pain." Jeannie eyed me. "Eighty and out, right?"

I grinned. "You said it, sister."

I was just about to tell her about the new boy I met when our parents came out. Mom was sniffling again, and Dad had his arm around her, telling her everything was going to be all right.

No one spoke on the way to the nursing home, and as we pulled in, I felt a wave of sadness wash over me that hadn't hit before. In the past, I'd complained about visiting Aunt Violet, but now that I knew how important she had been to my mom, I felt the weight of her loss.

We stepped out of the car. "I can't do this," Mom said, choking back tears.

Her tears triggered mine, but I wiped them from my face and took her hand. "We're going to do it together."

She looked at me, no longer having to look down because I had grown taller. "Okay."

A woman at the front desk had some papers for her to sign, and as she handled that, I glanced around, wondering how all these people ended up here and if they could possibly find happiness in a place like this. As I considered their predicament, the woman in charge told us to follow her. She took us to Aunt Violet's room and pointed to a box. "We've gathered all Violet's belongings for you," she said. "We thought it might make it easier."

Mom nodded. "May we have a moment before we go?"

"Of course," the woman said, leaving and closing the door behind her.

I watched as Mom wordlessly scanned the walls, gazed out the window for a while, and then ran her finger across the railing of the bed.

She turned to Dad. "I'm ready," she whispered.

Dad picked up the box, and we left. On the way out, I made eye contact with an elderly woman. She wore a house dress with slippers and was hunched over, gripping her walker. She looked aggravated, like life had let her down.

I averted my gaze and decided never to set foot in a place like that ever again.

Later that night, after Dad and Jeannie had gone to bed, I got up to get a glass of water and found my mom in the living room, looking at Aunt Violet's things.

Mom pulled a framed photo out and set it on the table. The one of Aunt Violet and her husband, Irving. She grabbed the picture I liked of Aunt Violet in the gown. I took it from her.

"She looked like a movie star," I said.

Mom smiled. "She did, didn't she?"

I saw a brightly-colored silk scarf wound into a ball and pulled it out of the box. "This is pretty," I said.

"I bought that for her for Christmas a long time ago."

I studied the print closer. "You can try it on if you like," Mom said.

I wrapped it around my neck so it hung unevenly, then I flipped my hair and smiled. "What do you think?"

"It looks good on you. You should keep it," she said. "Something to remember her by."

"Thanks." I gave her a kiss and went back to my room.

I glanced at my reflection in the mirror. The scarf did look good on me. I decided to wear it to the movies with Jim. The diner! I was supposed to meet Jim and tell him if my parents would let me go to the movies with him. "Shoot," I said.

The next morning Jeannie and I were talking when she

asked, "What's wrong?"

"Nothing. It's just I was supposed to meet someone, and with everything that happened yesterday, I couldn't."

Jeannie's interest was piqued. "Who?"

"A guy."

"What guy?"

I smiled. I couldn't help it. "His name is Jim. He just moved here from New York."

Jeannie looked impressed. "How did you meet him?"

I told her the story. "He sounds great," she said. "But what are you going to do now? He was probably waiting for you and thinks you blew him off."

The irony of how that had happened wasn't lost on me, making me feel worse. I didn't want him to think I wasn't interested in him or trying to teach him a lesson for joking about calling Sandy.

"I don't think it's a good time to ask Mom," I said. "I've never been on a date before, and now with Aunt Violet passing..." I sighed.

"You're going to have to ask Dad," Jeannie said.

"He's not going to go for it."

"He will if you say Bernice is going with. Or just say you're going to a movie with her and go with Jim instead."

Jeannie was only thirteen-years-old, but she was already advanced in the thinking-quick-on-her-feet department.

"Good ideas," I said.

Dad was in the bathroom, combing his hair.

"Hey, Dad. Can I talk to you for a minute?"

"Sure, honey. What's up?"

I was nervous but figured I'd try being honest. "A boy asked me to go to the movies with him, and I wanted to know if that was okay?"

Dad's expression grew serious. "Wow," he said, rubbing his chin. "We're at that point already, huh?"

"Guess so."

He was quiet for a minute, and during the silence, I wondered if I should have listened to Jeannie.

"Tell you what," he said. "Let me run it past your mother first."

That was never a good sign. It was a guaranteed no.

I went outside and sulked. At least I tried, I thought. When I returned home, Mom was sitting in the kitchen having coffee. She set her cup down when I came into the room.

"Your father tells me a boy asked you on a date."

"Yeah. His name is Jim. He just moved here from New York. He seems nice," I said.

Mom smiled faintly. "You're growing up, Lou. It makes me happy and sad at the same time."

I glanced down, unsure what to say. She was quiet for a while, then said, "I guess it would be all right if you went to a movie, but that's it. No drive-in movies or drag racing or riding in cars with boys. Understood?"

"Understood," I repeated. Riding in a car with a boy meant the end of a good reputation. I would never take a chance and do something stupid like that.

Chapter 10

After fussing over my hair and donning my prettiest dress, I headed to the soda shop. Though it was the wrong day, I showed up at the time Jim and I had agreed on in case he was there. I scanned the diner but didn't see him. My heart sank.

"You stood me up," a voice said from behind me.

I turned and found Jim leaning against the counter, smiling. He looked even better than the first time I had seen him.

"I've got a good excuse," I replied, wearing my cutest pout.

"I figured you were trying to give me a taste of my own medicine."

"Nope. Nothing like that. There was a death in the family."

"Oh. That's awful," he said, looking genuinely saddened. "I'm sorry to hear it."

"Thanks. It was my mom's aunt. She was eighty-four years old, so at least she lived a long life."

He nodded. "You wanna share a malt? It might make you feel better."

I smiled. "Sounds good."

We sat in an available booth, and he told the waiter our order. I felt comfortable around him even though we'd just met.

Our shake arrived. "They're starting to know me here. Three days in a row." He grinned, taking a sip from his straw.

I leaned in and sipped from mine.

"I'm hoping you've got good news from your parents?" he asked.

"Surprisingly, I do. They agreed to let me go to the movies with you, but it came with conditions."

Jim sat up straight. "What kind of conditions?"

"They said I could go to the movies with you, but no drive-in movies, no riding in the car with you, and no drag racing."

"No drag racing?" He looked disappointed. "And here I've got a Matador Red '57 Chevy Bel Air. What a shame."

I couldn't believe he had such a nice car. No one I knew had one. "Well, Mom didn't say anything about being a spectator."

"Don't worry. You won't have to break any of your parent's rules. I don't race my car. I've got more important things to do with my time, like make money to take you to the movies."

I lit up. It felt good to be thought of as important.

"When would you like to go?" he asked.

"Well, the funeral is tomorrow, and I should probably hang around the house. My mom has been really sad — she needs someone to cheer her up. Is Saturday afternoon good?"

"Saturday's perfect. I'd offer to give you a ride, but since you're not allowed, let's meet in front of the theater at noon."

"Okay," I said, smiling brightly. "I should be going home now. I told my mom I wouldn't be gone long."

"So soon?" Jim offered an exaggerated frown. "Okay, see you Saturday then."

"See you," I said as I stood. "And thanks for the malt."

"My pleasure," he said in a velvety voice.

I floated out the door, and once I was down the street, began skipping. I couldn't wait to see Bernice and tell her all the news. So much had changed in a few short days.

When I got home, I barged into Jeannie's room and jumped on her bed. "I'm so excited," I said.

Jeannie looked groggy. "That's swell, but can you please not shake the bed?"

"Why? What's wrong?"

"I got my period. Being a woman isn't as fun as I thought it would be." She frowned.

I remembered my first one. The cramps were excruciating. "Do you want me to get you some aspirin?"

She shook her head. "Already took some. Just waiting for the pain to go away." She fluffed her pillow, trying to get comfortable again. "So tell me what's going on."

"I went to see if the guy who asked me out was around, and he was. I told him Mom said I could go to the movies with him, and now we have a date for this weekend."

Jeannie's eyes grew wide. "Mom agreed to that?"

"Yep."

"Well, at least someone gets to do fun things around here," she said with a smirk.

I wasn't sure why she was reacting like that. There had never been any hostility between us.

"What do you mean?" I asked.

She sighed. "There's a boy I like, too. And when I hinted about going on a date with him, Mom immediately shut me down."

"What do you mean there's a boy you like? When did this happen? Geez. I thought you told me everything."

"I didn't tell you because he's a little older."

"How much older?"

"Over eighteen."

I raised an eyebrow. "How much over eighteen?"

"He's nineteen."

Her news had trumped my exciting news, but I didn't mind. I wanted her to tell me everything, and from the way she was acting, it seemed I'd have to pull it out of her bit by bit.

"Mom's not going to let you go out with a guy yet, especially not one over eighteen."

"I know. That's why I left that part out. I just said a boy had asked me to go to a movie. I figured you were going to ask, so maybe it would work for me, too."

"Yeah. But I'm a few years older than you, and even then, it was like they were going to say no."

"I'm almost fourteen," Jeannie added.

"Like that makes a difference to Mom and Dad." I shook my head at her. She had guts. I'd give her that. "Tell me more about him. How'd you meet a guy so old?"

"He's not old," Jeannie snapped.

"You know what I mean."

Jeannie hesitated. "He works at Smith's Auto Shop."

"Okay. But how do you know him? You said he asked you out."

"I talked to him once when I was there with Dad. He came around with the keys while Dad was in the restroom, and we got to chatting."

"Did Dad see?"

"No."

"What's his name?" I asked. She was being unusually guarded about him, and I didn't like it.

"Chuck," she said, smiling. "He's really nice. And dreamy, with blonde hair and blue eyes."

"And just like that, he asked you out?"

"Yep."

I frowned. But maybe Mom was right this time. Maybe she was too young to date, especially someone his age.

Jeannie looked at me. "Can you keep a secret?"

"Of course."

She glanced over my shoulder at the bedroom door, making sure it was shut, and lowered her voice. "Next time I was at the shop, I told Chuck the bad news. He said he was heartbroken we couldn't go on a date but understood."

I wanted to roll my eyes at how corny that line was but didn't because it would hurt Jeannie's feelings.

"One day, I was walking home from school, and he saw me and offered to give me a ride, so I accepted. He didn't drop me off here, though, just nearby so I wouldn't get into trouble."

My jaw dropped.

"Don't worry," she said. "Mom and Dad don't know."

I wasn't worried about them. I was worried about who might have seen her get into the car with him. Jeannie might have scammed our parents, but what she didn't realize was that she was already in deep shit.

Chapter 11

Aunt Violet's funeral was the most depressing day of my life. Mom cried harder than I'd ever seen her cry, Dad did his best to stay strong for her, and Jeannie was suffering from a severe case of diarrhea and had to keep escaping to the restroom.

I stood in front of the casket, feeling numb. Aunt Violet didn't seem real to me. She looked more like a made-up doll than the woman I visited at the old folks' home.

After saying a prayer, I turned toward my family and wiped a fake tear from my eye in the hopes I'd seem like a normal person. People were supposed to cry at funerals, not zone out. Thankfully everyone was so wrapped up in their own grief no one questioned the sincerity of my sadness.

The next day was Saturday, and I couldn't have been happier. I was dolled up and about to hop on my bike to meet Jim when my dad stopped me.

"How about I give you a ride," he said. "I wouldn't want you to show up out of breath and sweaty on your first date."

I thanked him and got in the car. As I sat there, I began to wonder if this was just a ploy to have "the talk."

My dad broke the somewhat awkward silence at a stoplight. "I remember my first date with your mom. Seems like it was yesterday."

So far, so good. "Where did you go?" I asked.

"A dance," he said, smiling. "She was the prettiest girl in school, and when I asked her, I didn't think she'd say yes, but she did."

"Guess you have to put yourself out there when you're a guy. Sounds stressful."

Dad turned the corner. "It can be."

We continued driving. When we pulled to the curb near the theater, he said, "Lou, I'm sure you know how boys are. You're not a child."

I felt my neck muscles tense. "Yes, Dad, I do. Mom told me all about it."

"Good," he said, looking relieved. "That saves me from having to tell you then. It's kind of awkward being a parent sometimes."

His honesty surprised me. "I hope I have the opportunity to find out someday."

"Me, too. But not too soon," he quickly added.

I shook my head. "Don't worry, Dad."

He nodded, and I stepped out. After I shut the door, he waved and drove away. I smoothed my dress, laughing to myself over how funny parents could be, and heard the sound of an engine rumbling. I watched as Jim pulled up, his Bel Air so clean it sparkled.

He parked and got out. He was wearing a white t-shirt and jeans. A husband and wife slowed to admire his car as they passed, and another man nodded at him in approval. Jim looked across the street and spotted me. A wide smile spread across his face as he crossed over. "Louise. You look beautiful," he said.

"Thank you." It was exactly the kind of thing I hoped to hear a man say to me someday. "You look nice, too." I pointed at his car. "And those wheels! You must get stopped everywhere you go."

Jim swelled with pride. "We do get a lot of attention. Maybe because I take such good care of her."

I could only imagine how great a husband he'd make if he took care of a car that well. He led the way inside and paid for our tickets, and I suddenly began to feel nervous.

"Would you like popcorn?" he asked.

"Only if you're having some." My answer sounded mousey, not at all like me, but I was feeling frazzled.

Jim got popcorn and soda, and we made our way through the semi-darkened theater to find good seats. An area was emptier than the others, and he chose to sit there, which made my heart race. I'd heard stories of boys expecting all kinds of things and hoped I wouldn't be put in a position where I would have to say no.

We began snacking on our food as we waited for the place to fill up. I wanted to say something to try and get to know him better, but my mouth was dry, and I couldn't think straight. I took a sip of soda. "How did you manage to get a car like that?"

"It's stolen," he said, wearing a straight face.

I studied him, trying to see if he was joking. He burst out laughing.

"I'm kidding," he said. "You should see the look on your face right now. It's adorable."

I laughed, which helped ease the tension. Beautiful. Adorable. I could get used to being called these names.

"So, are you going to tell me?" I asked again.

"I worked hard and saved up. I've been helping my dad with his business since I was a kid. Between what I saved and what he chipped in, we made it happen."

I couldn't help but notice the similarity to Bernice. She was motivated like that. "Boy. You must have really wanted that car."

"Yep. And if you really want something, I think you shouldn't stop trying until you get it."

With that said, the lights went out, and the previews started. I tried to focus on them but found myself preoccupied with sitting next to Jim. I'd just told my dad not to worry but was now sitting next to someone who had just admitted to the relentless pursuit of what he wanted.

The movie started, and thankfully nothing happened, so I relaxed into my seat and got absorbed in the plot. Then, about halfway through the film, Jim reached over and took hold of my hand. His was warm and dry and soft, and I didn't feel like pulling away, so I didn't.

Besides, holding hands was harmless. Everyone knew that.

My heart skipped as I wondered what he might try next. Part

of me hoped he would kiss me, and another part of me wanted to keep my word to my dad. Luckily, I didn't have to decide. When the credits rolled, all Jim had done was hold my hand for half of the film.

It was a sunny day, so we went for a walk in the park afterward. It was a shame we couldn't have driven there in his beautiful car, but we were stuck on foot as some rules couldn't be broken.

"What kind of business does your father have?" I asked him.

"He had two businesses. An apartment building and a Laundromat. But he sold them both, and we moved here."

By the tone of his voice, it sounded like there was a story behind that decision, but I didn't want to be nosy, so we continued walking, enjoying the sounds of birds happily chirping overhead.

An old couple sitting on a park bench caught my eye. Jim noticed them, too. "That's how it's supposed to turn out," he said. His words had a sharp edge to them, and as I looked at his face, I could see pain in his eyes. "My parents are divorced. That's why we came here…to get away from it all."

Divorced? I didn't know anyone whose parents were divorced. I didn't know what to say.

"My dad said he's going to start over. Get another Laundromat, buy another building." He looked into the distance, as if seeing the future they'd planned.

"I'm sure you'll help him be successful again," I said.

Jim turned to me. "I will." He smiled.

He glanced at my lips, and I thought he was going to kiss me, but he didn't. "We should be getting back," he said. "I'm sure your dad is worried sick waiting for you."

"How did you know?" I teased.

"Because I make a habit of observing people. I can tell my dad worries about me all the time, even though he never says it. Plus, I'm a guy," he smirked. "Your dad probably thinks I've tried to have my way with you."

I blushed. "We did have *the talk* on the way here," I said.

Jim laughed. "I'll bet."

He reached for my hand, and I laced my fingers through his as we headed back to his car.

"Thanks for the movie and the popcorn," I said. "I had fun on my first date."

Jim stopped. "This is the first date you've been on?"

"Uh-huh," I replied nervously.

We got to his car and faced each other. "Well, I'm honored I could be your first date. How did I do?"

I blushed. "I can't think of how it could have been any better."

Jim stepped closer. He gazed deep into my eyes and said, "Me neither." He gave me a kiss on the cheek, hopped in his car, and drove away.

Chapter 12

The next day I walked to Bernice's house, my mind buzzing with all that had happened since we saw each other last.

Her mom answered the door. "How's your arm?" I asked her, noticing her artwork covered cast.

She lifted it. "Healing...in style."

I smiled, and Bernice came in.

"What's new?" she asked.

"Tons. We need to talk." We went outside and began walking to the park.

"Let me start with the bad news. Aunt Violet died."

"Oh no! Your mom must be so upset."

"She is. But I think it's for the best because Aunt Violet was in a lot of pain."

Bernice kicked a large pebble. "True."

"And now for the good news. I met a boy named Jim. He just moved here from New York." I paused and added, "We went on a date."

Bernice stopped walking. "No way."

"Yep." I beamed. "He's really nice. I think you'll like him."

"He sounds great," she said, but she wasn't very enthusiastic.

I didn't expect her to jump up and down, but this was a big moment. "How come you don't seem happy for me?" I asked.

"I am," she assured me. "I guess my mind is elsewhere. Sorry."

"What's going on?"

She exhaled noisily. "It's this college thing. There just aren't very many options for women, and that's so frustrating."

"Can you major in business like you hoped?"

"I can major in whatever they think is appropriate for me, not what I want."

"But you're paying tuition. Doesn't that mean you have a say?"

Bernice laughed blackly. "You'd think so, but no. They'll take our money, but they still run the show."

There was nothing worse in the world for Bernice than being told she couldn't do something she'd set out to do. Her mind was probably working around the clock to find a way to overcome the obstacle.

"But there's still hope, right? Surely there are some schools that let women study business?"

"Yeah. But the list is narrowing. Some of the more progressive schools are out of state."

We sat on the swings, but I didn't start swinging. My happiness had deflated like someone let the air out of a balloon.

"Gosh, I hope you don't have to leave," I said.

"I might have to." She looked down.

I didn't want to think about it right now. "Let's go get a soda. My treat," I offered.

"Okay."

We raced each other to the soda shop and spent a long time chatting while sipping our drinks. Then I saw Jim pull up. When he got out, a few pretty girls came his way, oohing and ahhing over his car, trying to make conversation with him.

Bernice noticed my attention had drifted. "Is that your boyfriend?" she asked.

I didn't take my eyes from the scene. "We just went on one date."

Jim was talkative but not flirtatious. His body language didn't indicate he was interested in any of them, which surprised me since they were all much more popular than me.

He walked inside, and when he spotted Bernice and me, he came our way.

"Hey, Lou," he said, wearing a big smile.

"Hey." I smiled back. Bernice looked uncomfortable all of a sudden, like she wanted to disappear.

"Who's your friend?" Jim asked.

"This is my best friend, Bernice."

"Hello," she said, offering a little wave.

"Pleased to meet you. Anyone who can be called Lou's best friend must be someone special."

Bernice and I smiled in agreement.

"Do you want to join us?" I asked him.

"No thanks. I'm just picking up dinner for my dad and me."

I pictured him and his recently divorced father sitting at the kitchen table together. The thought warmed me.

"Okay. See you around then," I said, trying to act casual.

Jim placed his order and stopped by again on his way out. "I'm not sure if you'd be interested, but there's a dance coming up soon. Would you like to go with me?"

He stood holding his to-go order, looking nervous.

"Of course," I answered. "But let me run it by my parents just to be sure."

Jim turned to Bernice. "I've got a few friends who don't have dates yet. Do you think you'd be able to help me out with that?"

Bernice looked taken aback. "I don't know. I've been really busy lately," she finally managed.

"Understood," Jim said.

With that said, he left, and when he was out the door, I turned to Bernice. "That was the lamest excuse I've ever heard."

She shrugged. "I'm not good with being put on the spot."

"I can tell," I smirked. "But really, why don't you come with us? It'll be fun."

Bernice looked unconvinced. "I don't think so."

"Give me one good reason not to go."

She began fiddling with her straw. "Because I should be studying," she said.

"That's not good enough. You'll have to do better."

Bernice narrowed her eyes. "Because I don't want to get

involved with anyone. I don't want to take a chance I might fall head over heels for someone like you obviously have and then have to leave the state for school."

"What, so you're not going to go on any dates until you graduate?" I asked.

"No."

The idea seemed silly, but I knew better than to push her as she rarely changed her mind.

"What about if he sets you up with the ugliest kid he knows?"

Bernice choked on her soda. She managed to swallow it and let out a laugh. "That's awful, Lou. What if the guy really liked me? That wouldn't be right."

"You're a party-pooper, you know that?"

"So I've been told."

"Well, if you change your mind, let me know."

Bernice smiled. "I won't."

"I know, but I wish you would. We need to have as much fun as possible in case you go away for four years."

Later on, I told my mom I'd do the dinner dishes. I plopped down on the sofa opposite my dad when I had finished.

He was sitting in his favorite chair, reading the paper.

"How's work been?" I asked.

"Fine," he replied.

He just sat there, staring at me.

"Is there something you want to talk about?" he asked.

I shifted in my seat. "I just wanted to hear how things have been at your job," I replied unconvincingly. "You know, find out about the office."

"I'm a pipefitter," Dad snickered. "I don't sit at a desk."

"I knew that." This was going bad fast. I decided I better get to the point and not dig myself a deeper hole.

"Did you want to talk about something else?" He looked anxious to get back to his paper.

I cut to the chase. "Yeah, I do want to talk to you about

something else. Jim asked me to the school dance, but I told him I had to check with you first."

Dad smiled. As he thought it over, time seemed to stop.

"I don't see why not," he finally answered.

Chapter 13

Jim was a grade higher than me, so I hadn't seen him at school yet but hoped I'd bump into him today so I could tell him the good news.

I craned my neck to see if the guy in the center of a group of girls was him when Frankie came into my field of vision, his freckled face ugly as ever.

"Hey, Lou. How's your sister?" He was smiling, but his tone was accusatory, not conversational.

I wasn't in the mood for his crap, so I ignored him.

"Tell her I'm getting a car soon and that she's welcome to go for a ride."

That comment stopped me.

Recognition hit — and he knew that I knew.

I wanted to charge him, to go ballistic and slap him repeatedly until he begged for forgiveness. Instead, I smiled back, gave him the middle finger, and then walked away.

The rest of the day, I struggled to focus on school. And I didn't even bother looking for Jim because I was so angry. All I wanted to do was race home right when the bell rang so I could wring Jeannie's neck. I couldn't believe she had been so careless.

When I walked in, Jeannie was smiling, but her expression changed to concern once she saw me.

"What's wrong?" she asked.

Mom was nearby, so I motioned for her to follow me to my room. I shut the door and sat her down.

"How much do you trust this Chuck fellow?" I asked.

"I trust him completely. Why?"

The comment proved her naivety. "Because I think he's been telling someone about you and him. That's why."

She shook her head. "He wouldn't do that. He knows we have to wait until I'm older to be seen in public together. Right now, we're just getting to know each other. Nothing's happened. I swear."

"I thought you only saw him outside of work that one time?"

Jeannie scrunched her face. "Well…"

"Jesus Christ."

"Don't freak out, okay?" she said. "I'm in love with him. I just can't pretend he doesn't exist and have another girl get him because of bad timing."

I sighed. I could understand how she felt but was still upset. "And nothing has happened?"

Jeannie looked me in the eye. "We've kissed, but that's it."

This was going from bad to worse, but I didn't want to lose my cool since she had leveled with me. "Well, someone has either seen you in the car with him, or he's talked because that idiot Frankie was spreading rumors about you today."

Jeannie gasped. Then her forehead creased, the way it did right before she was going to start bawling. "He promised me he wouldn't tell anyone," she sniffled.

Seeing her hurting broke my heart. "Don't cry," I said in a soft voice. "It might not have been him. As I said, someone might have seen you together." I reached for her hand and gave it a gentle squeeze. "We'll fix this," I promised.

"How?"

That was the problem. I had no idea.

"You don't want to stop seeing him, right?" I asked.

She shook her head no.

I started biting my fingernail, trying to think. "Okay. Here's what we're going to do," I said, locking eyes with her. "We'll say it's a lie. Everyone knows Frankie hates me and would do anything to cause me grief. We have to get people believing he's just spreading gossip." I gave her a serious stare. "But that means, going forward, you can't go for rides in his car. If you're going to spend time together, you'll have to do it some other way."

Jeannie pouted. She clearly didn't like that part of the bargain. "But where can we go?"

"Mom and Dad won't let you date him yet, that's for sure. And with the car off-limits, that doesn't leave you many options. Could you go to his house?" I couldn't believe I had just suggested that, but she looked hopeless, and it was all I could think of at the moment.

Jeannie still looked worried.

"If it's meant to be, it will be," I said.

***

I saw Jim at school the next day.

"Hey." He smiled. "Did you talk to your dad?"

"I did. And he said yes. I was looking for you yesterday but got sidetracked."

"Decided to leave me hanging again, huh?" he teased. "I'm jealous of whatever was more important than getting back to me."

"Nothing to be jealous of," I assured him. "Just dealing with a problem."

He looked concerned. "Anything serious?"

"I'm not sure yet."

"Hmm…well, I don't want my girl having problems. Is there anything I can do to help?"

I hesitated. Then, as if he sensed my apprehension, he leaned closer and said, "You can trust me, Lou. If it's a secret, I promise I won't tell a soul."

I wavered, then decided I would tell him since he said I was his girl. "It's kind of a delicate matter," I whispered, then motioned for him to follow me to the hallway corner, away from potential eavesdroppers.

"You know that moron, Frankie?" Jim nodded. "Well, he's

been spreading rumors about my younger sister, Jeannie, saying she's been riding in the car with an older boy."

Jim smiled. "I think I can handle this for you," he said.

"I don't want you to beat him up. That'll just make it worse. People will think Jeannie's guilty, and her reputation is already in question—"

"Don't worry. I won't lay a finger on him. I'm going to handle it another way."

I gave him a puzzled look. "How?"

His smile widened. "I happen to have a little secret of my own. You know Betty?"

I nodded. Who didn't know Betty? She was the prettiest girl in school but not very nice.

"Well, Frankie has a massive crush on her. Since she's a friend of mine, I told him I'd help him out." I was about to speak when he said, "I know what you're thinking. Frankie doesn't have a chance with her. I know that. And you know that. But he doesn't. Frankie will do anything I say to get a date with her. I can pull his strings like a puppet. Trust me."

I'd never thought of Frankie having a human heart, much less being in love with someone. "If you say so," I said.

"Consider it handled," he concluded. Then he turned and went to class.

The day seemed to drag on indefinitely, and I was thankful when it was over. I was tired and couldn't wait to get home and take a nap. On the way out, a book slipped from my stack, and as I reached down to get it, someone had already scooped it up and was handing it to me. I straightened when I saw it was Frankie.

"Hey, Lou. I just wanted to come by and apologize for what I said about your sister. Someone was spreading rumors about her, and I shouldn't have gotten caught up in believing them."

I couldn't believe my ears and eyes. Frankie, right in front of me, being the very picture of contrite.

I played along. "Mistakes happen," I said.

He was still standing there. He looked like he wasn't sure if he'd done a good enough job of apologizing. I made eye contact.

"We're cool," I assured him.

That seemed to work because his shoulders relaxed, and he said, "Cool. See you around, Lou."

Betty passed by not long after. She was giggling about something one of her friends had said, completely oblivious to the impact she'd just made in my and Jeannie's lives. For all her crummy faults, I wanted to run up and give her a big hug. But I didn't. Instead, I went home and told Jeannie.

"Gosh. That's great, Lou. I knew you'd fix everything."

"It was Jim who did it," I told her, trying to play down my involvement.

"But it happened because of you," she said. "I owe you."

I waved her off. "You don't owe me anything. You'd do the same for me."

"True." She smiled, and I smiled too, feeling better knowing she was off the hook.

"So, have you talked to him?" I asked.

"I stopped by his work on my way home and told him what was going on. He said he had never told anyone and that maybe it was like you said. Someone had seen. Anyway, he gave me his address and asked if I could come over one day this weekend. He said his dad said it was okay. Will you cover for me? Say I'm with you?"

I knew it wasn't a particularly good idea, but Jeannie was hard to say no to. "Sure," I said. "No problem."

Chapter 14

Jim held my hand as we stood by the punchbowl, watching everyone on the dance floor. I was having a blast but wished Bernice had agreed to come along. But, true to form, she didn't change her mind even though I did my best to convince her. I scanned the room and saw Frankie dancing. Not with Betty, but with another, less attractive girl. He looked happy and had been surprisingly pleasant ever since Jim had that little discussion with him.

The song ended, and Elvis Presley's *It's Now or Never* came on. Jim had been sipping his drink but set it down and pulled me on the dance floor. We slowly swayed back and forth as the claves clicked their hypnotic rhythm, his arms wrapped around my waist and mine around his neck. Jim fixed me with an intense gaze as the King crooned, 'It's now or never.' And as the song ended, I found myself agreeing with Elvis, thinking that tomorrow would indeed be too late.

I whispered in Jim's ear, then slipped out the gymnasium side door when the teacher wasn't looking. I hid by the bushes, my heart hammering in my chest, both from the fear of getting caught and anticipation. A few minutes later, Jim showed up, and without a moment's hesitation, pulled me close to him and began kissing me, softly at first, then more passionately, exploring my mouth with his tongue.

I was lost in the moment when I heard a branch snap. Jim and I looked up and found a boy sneaking a cigarette. When he realized we were there, he whispered, "Sorry."

Jim turned back to me and smiled. "Where were we?"

"You were making my knees weak."

"Oh yeah," he said as he leaned in for another kiss.

We continued necking, and I was lost in a feeling I'd never

had before, like I was flying. He started putting his hand up my blouse when the gymnasium door swung open.

"I know there are several of you out here, and I suggest you return immediately," an elderly male voice ordered.

I groaned as the three of us hung our heads and walked inside. The boy returned to his friends, and Jim and I hit the dance floor, where we danced to a bunch of fast songs in a row. It was like I had limitless energy. I hoped the evening would never end.

The last song of the night was a slow one. Jim wrapped his arms around me, gazed into my eyes, and asked, "Will you go steady with me?"

"Of course," I answered.

I was already his, and he knew it. I was so excited, I wanted to shout his name from the rooftops. Outside, while waiting for my dad to pick me up, he turned to me. "I've got something for you." He slipped a chain with his school ring hanging on it over my head and smiled.

I beamed. "I'll never take it off."

He looked like he was going to kiss me again, which would have been a bad idea due to the teachers standing nearby. He glanced from side to side like he was considering it, but then my dad pulled up.

I leaned toward the open window. "Hey, Dad. I want to introduce you to my boyfriend, Jim."

Dad parked and got out. Jim went around to shake his hand. "Nice to meet you, sir," Jim said.

"Likewise. My daughter speaks very highly of you."

"I can't think of a better compliment," Jim said.

Jim nodded at my dad, then came over by me. "I had a great time," he said in a tone far more formal than velvet. Then he winked.

"Me, too," I said, giddy beyond belief and not trying to hide it.

As my dad and I drove away, I reached for Jim's ring. This

was the best night of my life, and I had never been so happy.

"What have you got there?" Dad asked.

He stopped at a red light, and I lifted the chain and showed him the ring.

"So it's official, huh?"

A wide smile spread across my face. "Yep."

"Why do you keep doing that?" my dad asked.

"Doing what?"

"Growing up."

I laughed, then we pulled in front of the house. "Thanks for letting me go to the dance. You're the best dad ever."

"You're welcome, sweetie. Jim seems like a nice guy. You should invite him to dinner soon."

"I will," I said, then ran to Jeannie's room.

She was sitting on her bed doing math homework but dropped her pencil when she saw me.

"How did it go?" she asked.

"He asked me to go steady." I showed her the ring.

"Ooh," she cooed as she sat up and reached for it. "That's swell." She gave me a sidelong glance. "Anything else happen?"

I told her about the Elvis song and the kissing. She jumped up and down and shrieked with delight. I joined her, and we broke into a fit of giggles.

Mom poked her head in. "Sounds like I'm missing all the fun," she said.

It was nice to see her smiling again.

I showed her the ring, and her smile widened as she examined it, nodding approval. "Well, I guess there is cause for celebration. This is a very big deal," she proclaimed.

"Dad said we should have him over for dinner soon."

"Invite him next weekend," she suggested, then rubbed the top of my head like she did when I was a kid and left.

My mom would always see me as her child, but I finally felt like an adult for the first time. I'd always wanted to grow up as quickly as possible so I could have control of my own life, and now I was a bit closer to my goal. The ring around my neck was proof.

I eyed Jeannie, still a little miffed she'd kissed a boy before I did. "You still need me to cover for you tomorrow?" I asked.

"Yeah. You don't mind, do you?"

I kind of did but had gotten in over my head. And a deal was a deal. "Of course not. Just do me a favor."

"What?"

"Don't make me regret this."

Jeannie looked hurt. "What do you mean?"

"You know what I mean. Don't go any further than kissing. I don't want to be the one that helped you out, and you end up in a bad way."

Jeannie took my hand. "I promise I won't let you down," she said.

The next day, we planned to meet at Bernice's house, then walk home together so it would look like we had been out playing all day. Bernice's mom had just made cookies, and we were looking at a magazine when I heard the doorbell ring.

"Hi. Is Lou here?" It was Jeannie's voice.

I checked my watch, wondering why she was so early, then went to the door to meet her. "What's wrong?" I asked.

"Everything," she said, her lower lip quivering.

"Hang on. Let me just go and say goodbye to Bernice, and then we'll head home."

Jeannie nodded, and when I returned, I handed her a warm cookie.

"What happened?" I asked when we left.

Jeannie burst into tears. "My life is ruined," she said.

My stomach dropped. If she were to get pregnant, my parents would kill me for playing along with her lie.

We stopped walking. Then I put my hand on her shoulder. "Tell me what happened."

Jeannie was crying so hard it was scaring me. "He's going to Vietnam," she said, then began crying some more.

I put my arms around her. "I'm so sorry."

"What if I never see him again?" she sobbed.

I didn't want to lie to her. "That's a possibility," I said. "But if it's meant to be, he'll come back in one piece."

Jeannie wiped the tears from her face with the back of her hand. "He asked me to wait for him. He said when he comes back, I'd be old enough to date, and then we wouldn't have to hide."

"And what did you say?" I asked.

"I told him I'd wait forever for him," she said.

I took her hands in mine. "Then let's pray he comes home."

Chapter 15

For the next few weeks, Jeannie behaved like a widow who had lost her husband. She stared into space, forlorn, and nothing I said or did seemed to cheer her up.

"What do you think is going on with Jeannie?" Mom asked me as we cleaned the house.

I finished wiping the coffee table and shrugged. "Who knows," I replied. If our parents knew why Jeannie was depressed, we would both be in a world of trouble.

"Maybe you can talk to her," she suggested. "It's pretty obvious that something is on her mind."

"I'll try," I said, spritzing the family room window with glass cleaner. I was glad my back was facing her because if she could see my face, she'd know I was hiding something.

"Thanks, honey. I tried to talk to her, but she told me everything was fine. I think anyone can see that's not true."

"If I find out what it is, you'll be the first to know." That seemed to satisfy her, and the subject was thankfully dropped.

Later that day, Jim told me his dad had bought an apartment building. He said he could use help cleaning the units, spackling and painting the walls, and asked Jim if any of his friends wanted to earn some extra money.

"Count me in," Bernice said as we sat in her room. "I could use all the money I can get my hands on for school."

She'd been kind of quiet about that lately. "So, what's the latest news on that front?"

"We found a few colleges that accept women into the business program."

"Any good ones?"

She hesitated. "Yeah. I made a decision."

"And?" I asked.

Bernice looked at me. "I'm going to go to UNM."

"Where's that?"

"It's the University of New Mexico."

"Oh." My stomach dropped as my face fell.

"My parents liked that I'd have family nearby. And that they're progressive. They've had a women's basketball team since 1889."

I nodded, suddenly unable to speak.

"And Juan knows someone who's gone there. He said it's a good school and that I'm going to love Albuquerque."

I managed a smile. "That's great news. Really."

Bernice put a hand on my shoulder. "It's only four years. I'll be back in no time."

"I know. But I'm going to miss you."

"More like I'll miss you, and you'll be busy having so much fun with Jim you won't even know I'm gone," she joked.

That brought on a small smile. "Yeah...and what about Juan's older brother?"

"Alejandro?" She seemed surprised I remembered him.

"Uh-huh." I grinned.

"I doubt I'll see him again. Juan said he took a job in Arizona."

"Bummer. Well, it's best to stay focused on school anyway, right?"

"Right."

I knew it was childish, but part of me was envious she was getting to go out west. Then I thought of Chuck and how he'd been sent halfway around the world to fight in a jungle and realized I was an idiot, that I should be thankful for the life I had.

"You should come and visit me," Bernice said, interrupting my thought.

"That's a good idea," I said, already getting excited about it. "It will be like the trip we didn't get to take, only better because we're older."

"Yep. We can do all kinds of fun stuff. And you can finally

meet Juan and my aunt. It'll be a blast."

With that settled, things didn't seem so bad. She might be going away to school, but we would have something to look forward to.

Over the next few months, Bernice and I kept busy helping Jim's dad on weekends. I'd convinced Jeannie to work with us, hoping it would take her mind off Chuck.

"He hasn't written," Jeannie said as she peeled the faded wallpaper.

"How can he? If he sent a letter to the house, Dad would wonder why his old mechanic is writing his daughter," I said.

Jeannie sighed. Having a secret relationship continued to be complicated even though he was gone. "Well, it would be nice to know how he's doing, you know, and if he's still alive."

Bernice had just opened a can of paint. "If he was hurt, wouldn't someone in his family contact you?" she asked.

"No," she said. "His dad never met me, so he wouldn't know to tell me."

I picked up a paint brush, dipped it in the pan, and began edging the molding. "I thought you met his dad?"

"I never got to meet him. He was at work when I stopped by."

I raised an eyebrow, wondering if Chuck's dad even knew Jeannie had been over. Maybe it was a good thing Chuck had been sent away. Knowing how I reacted when Jim kissed me, it was easy to guess where things might have gone between Chuck and Jeannie if he was still around.

"It doesn't make sense to wait for a guy if you didn't know whether he's dead or alive," said Bernice. She turned to face us. "I have an idea. How about you ask Jim to take his car to the shop where Chuck used to work for a tune-up? He can ask for Chuck and say your dad referred him. Then, when they say he doesn't work there anymore, he can get them talking about him. Someone's bound to know something, right?"

"Oh my God! That's genius," Jeannie said. "Why didn't I

think of that?"

"Because you're too close to the problem," Bernice explained. "Trust me. I've been there."

"Do you think Jim will do it?" Jeannie asked, looking eager.

I thought about it for a moment. "I don't see why not. I'll ask him when he gets here."

Jim arrived shortly after Jeannie and Bernice had left. It was just the two of us in the empty apartment building surrounded by tarps and painting supplies. He surveyed the walls and nodded.

"The place looks great," he said. Then he came closer, his eyes filled with desire.

I had wanted him for so long and had wished we could be alone somewhere, and now that we were, I felt shy, like a little girl playing at being an adult. I feared he'd see right through me and laugh. Instead, he held my gaze and dropped to one knee.

"I know you've got one year of school left, but I want you to marry me, Louise. What do you say?"

I gulped. It didn't get any more grown-up than that. "Yes!" I said.

He scooped me in his arms and spun me around. The room became a blur as I giggled with delight, then he set me down, cradled my face in his hands, and kissed me. Jim didn't own a black horse and live out west, but I loved him with all of my heart.

His kiss grew more passionate, and then we were pawing at each other, breathing heavily. We hadn't had sex yet, but now that we were engaged... I pulled away and looked him in the eye. "I think I'm ready," I said.

Jim gazed at me through heavy lids and then, without a word, began unbuttoning my blouse. When he had finished, he tossed it to the floor and pulled his sweater over his head. We stared at each other for a beat, then continued where we left off.

Things got hot and heavy quickly. Jim pulled away and

glanced around the room. "All we've got is an empty room with hardwood floors," he groaned.

"I don't care," I said, short of breath.

I unbuttoned my skirt, and it fell to the floor, then I kicked it aside as Jim stripped out of his jeans. He picked me up and laid me down on the paint-splattered tarp. He continued kissing me, focusing on my neck, and then worked his way down.

I had heard sex would hurt the first time and had prepared myself for something less than wonderful. But, to my surprise, it only hurt for a few minutes, then it felt good and got progressively better. Feeling Jim's weight on top of me and listening to the sounds he made gave me a feeling of satisfaction I had never known. I didn't even mind the strong smell of paint.

When it was over, Jim kissed me and smiled. "I love you, Lou," he said in his velvety voice.

I was hit by a powerful wave of emotion, which culminated in a single tear rolling down my cheek. "I love you too, Jim. So much."

Chapter 16

Jim asked me not to mention our engagement to anyone until he could get a ring. He said his dad knew a guy in New York who knew a guy here who could get him a great deal on a diamond, so he would stop by his place after school. He'd also scheduled an appointment to have his car tuned up at the shop where Chuck used to work so he could help Jeannie.

With everything that was going on, I could barely focus at school. The teacher called on me to answer a question, and I had spaced out, unsure which page we were on. My classmates' laughter brought me back to the present, and I managed to stumble through.

Once I'd finished dinner and my homework, I heard the doorbell ring. Mom answered it. "Lou. Jim's here," she called out.

I jumped up and raced to meet him. He stood there grinning ear to ear.

"You're in a good mood," I said as I stepped outside.

"I am." He pulled a small box out of his jacket. "I bought a ring for the most amazing girl." He opened the box. "What do you think?"

I gasped. "Oh, Jim…it's beautiful!" I had expected a band with a small diamond. This stone was much larger than that.

He slipped it on my finger. "You're my fiancé now," he purred. Then he gave me a kiss. "You want to share the news?"

"Yes," I said giddily, taking another glance at my finger.

Jim and I went inside. Mom, Dad, and Jeannie were glued to the TV, engrossed in an episode of *The Twilight Zone*, so we sat in the kitchen and munched on some cookies, waiting for the show to end. Jim and I sat opposite each other, and the energy in the room was palpable.

Jim seemed pleased that I liked the ring. I thought the ring was beautiful but was more excited to be officially engaged. All I could think of was the apartment we would share and his job taking care of all the tenants. He said I could pick out whatever furniture I wanted. It was like all my dreams were coming true at once. Well, except perhaps for the western dream – but I was beginning to believe that had just been a childhood fantasy.

"What's going on?" Jeannie asked. I'd been so immersed in my daydreams I hadn't realized she'd come into the room.

I lifted my hand, and her eyes popped. "Oh my God!" she gasped.

"What's all the excitement about?" Dad asked as he made his way to the kitchen, Mom following right behind him.

Jim and I stood up.

"Mom. Dad. We have an announcement. Jim and I are getting married," I told them. Then I thrust my hand out so they could see the ring.

My dad looked like he was going to say something, like he thought I was too young still, but one look at the diamond and his jaw dropped.

"This is wonderful news," Mom chimed in, looking as excited as I felt.

Jim smiled at her. She was the hardest person to win over, and he'd managed to charm her from day one.

"Thank you," he said. "I'm glad you feel that way. I happen to think I'm the luckiest man alive."

Dad reached out to shake Jim's hand. "Well done," he said. "I'll be proud to have you as a son-in-law."

Jim stood a little straighter. "Thank you. I'd be honored to call you Dad."

We talked for a while about our plans for the future, and from the looks on my parents' faces, I could tell they were pleased. Jim was one of those rare young men who had his stuff together.

When my parents had gone to bed, Jeannie came and sat next to me. "I'm so happy for you," she said. "I can't think of a better husband for my big sister."

I was thrilled Jeannie liked him. It would've been awful to marry a guy she couldn't stand.

"He's good to me," I said.

Jeannie looked me in the eye. "He's good to me, too. I really appreciate his help."

"Let's hope he's got some good news about Chuck after he visits the shop tomorrow."

She nodded, her expression hopeful.

The next day, I made a point to pay attention in class even though my mind was filled with mushy daydreams, bridal gowns, and ideas for decorating our future apartment. Jim and I had agreed to get married after school was out. He'd graduate, but I'd finish my last year as a married woman, which I didn't mind one bit.

I told Bernice about my engagement and showed her the ring at lunch.

"It's gorgeous!" she exclaimed. "Congratulations!"

"Thanks." I unwrapped my sandwich. "We're having a small wedding at the courthouse, just close family, but I want you to be there."

"Wouldn't miss it." She took a sip of milk. "I'm glad you're getting married before I leave for college. I was worried it may happen afterward, and I'd have to find a way to make it back."

"Happy to help," I told her, then bit into my food.

After school, Bernice and I took the bus to Polk Brothers to look at furniture. We'd come a long way from pitching pennies together, and as we sat on the bus discussing our favorite sofa styles, I smiled.

"What are you smiling about?" she asked.

"Just savoring the moment."

Bernice understood and smiled too. Our time together was limited. We needed to savor every moment left.

When we got to the store, an older gentleman greeted us. He was polite but didn't seem interested in showing us around until

I said my fiancé sent me on a mission to decorate our new home.

"Let me give you the store tour," he said, his eyes taking on a new sparkle when he spotted my ring.

Bernice and I listened as he described the quality of their furniture. We sat in a dozen sofas, and I made a mental note of which ones I thought were the most comfortable and attractive.

The salesman pulled out a pen and said, "I can jot down your favorites if you like."

"That would be wonderful," I replied. I giggled when I realized I'd sounded just like my mother.

When we'd finished, he gave us some brochures to take home. "That way, you and your fiancé can make a decision together." I shook his hand, promising to contact him as soon as we were ready to buy.

Bernice and I went our separate ways when we got off the bus, and as I got closer to home, I noticed Jim's car parked out front. I ran toward him. I couldn't wait to show him the brochures from the furniture store.

"What's wrong?" I asked when I saw his face.

He looked down. "I just got back from picking up my car."

I'd been so wrapped up in shopping I'd completely forgotten about that. "And?" I asked, hoping for good news.

"And no one has heard from Chuck."

"What does that mean?"

Jim crossed his arms in front of his chest and furrowed his brow. "It means he hasn't written them, or the guys at the shop don't talk to his dad."

"But it doesn't mean he's...?"

Jim let out a deep exhale. "It could mean that."

"But if that happened, wouldn't someone have told the guys that work there?"

"Not necessarily. If you were a parent and found out your kid died, you'd be devastated. You might not tell everyone. Only close family."

I gripped the brochures as I tried to think. "We have to come up with another way to find out then because I can't leave Jeannie hanging."

"Agreed. I've only been waiting here for ten minutes, but right when I pulled up, Jeannie came out and asked me what I'd heard."

"How did she take it?" Of course, I already knew the answer.

"Not well."

"Shit," I said. "I'd better go to her." I gave him a quick kiss on the lips and started toward the door. "Thank you. See you tomorrow?"

"Tomorrow," he repeated, smiling.

I waved at Mom, who was in the kitchen frying onions, and headed to my room. I threw the furniture store pamphlets on the bed, then went to Jeannie's room and knocked softly on the door.

"Come in," she said in a quiet voice.

I entered and noticed she had been crying. I quickly closed the door. Jeannie looked up at me. She didn't have to say the words. I knew that expression well.

I reached over and gave her a hug. "I'm going to find out about Chuck. I promise."

Jeannie pulled back and looked at me. "I know," she said. "If anyone can find out, it's you."

Chapter 17

I spent the rest of the night trying to figure out how I would keep my promise to Jeannie. When we were young, her problems were easier to fix. I could be the big sister she expected me to be. Now that we were getting older, it was more challenging, and I woke the next morning no closer to having the solution than when I went to bed.

After breakfast, I headed to Bernice's house, hoping she might have an idea. I knocked on her door and then rubbed my temples in an attempt to alleviate the throbbing pain in my head.

Bernice answered. "What's going on?" she asked. "Is everything okay between you and Jim?"

"We're good," I said as I walked inside. "I'm just worried about Jeannie."

I told her about Jim's fruitless trip to the repair shop after we sat down, and she frowned.

"So much for me being a genius," she scoffed. Then she pursed her lips and began tapping her fingers on her knee. "Does Chuck's family know who you are?"

"Not that I know of. Why?"

Bernice described her plan.

"It could work," I said.

"Do you want me to come with you?"

"No. I think I can do it on my own."

Jeannie gave me Chuck's address after I filled her in on what Bernice had suggested. Then I explained it all to Jim, and he agreed to drop me off nearby so I could approach the house on foot. In the meantime, I practiced the lines in my mind.

I rang the buzzer and waited, but no one answered. I considered leaving but couldn't give up so easily. After a reasonable amount of time had passed, I rang the buzzer again.

The door swung open after the second ring. "Persistent, aren't you," said a man with disheveled hair and a grumpy expression.

I hadn't rehearsed a response to that greeting. "Hello," I tried to say in an upbeat tone.

"Not interested," the man grumbled, then began closing the door.

"But I haven't even said why I'm here."

"You're selling something. I'm not buying."

"I'm not selling something. I'm here from school."

The man looked confused.

I held up the pad of paper I had brought and took the cap off my pen. "I'm with the school newspaper," I told him. "We're doing a story on recent graduates to see what they're doing now. You have a son named Chuck, right?"

The man crossed his arms in front of his chest. "I do."

"Well, we'd like to know how he's doing. If he's working, away in college..."

There was a moment of silence that seemed to last forever. The man appeared to be considering my question as he studied me.

"Do you have any ID to prove you're affiliated with the school?"

"No," I mumbled, inwardly cursing that I hadn't thought of that.

"Well, then I don't feel comfortable discussing my son with you."

He started closing the door, so I blurted, "Hold on. Let me explain."

He paused, looking highly annoyed.

"Okay. I'm going to level with you. I don't work for the school. But I am a student there."

The man raised his eyebrow.

"Here's the real story. My younger sister has a secret crush on your son. She met him at the auto shop. Since he left for

Vietnam, she's been worried sick, so I told her I'd find out how he's doing without letting anyone in on her secret."

The man's expression softened, and he dropped his arms to his side. "Guess you kind of blew that promise, huh?"

I nodded, embarrassed beyond words. The plan had gone from bad to worse.

"Well, if I wasn't a cop, you might've fooled me. The school newspaper story was a pretty good ruse."

My face flushed red, and I managed a smile. "I should have just been honest from the start."

The man chuckled. "Don't sweat it." Then he rubbed his unshaven face, looking like he was trying to decide if he wanted to talk to me. And as he did so, I noticed his eyes had dark circles beneath them.

"How about I level with you too," he said, holding my gaze. "After Chuck left, he wrote a couple of times, then stopped. My gut told me to be concerned, and sure enough, soon afterward, I got a phone call saying he was missing in action."

"I...I don't know what to say," I replied in a hushed tone. "That's terrible."

Chuck's dad nodded. "Now you know why I was reluctant to discuss my son. I'm only telling you so you can tell your sister."

My heart sank. "I don't know how I'm going to tell her this. She's been waiting for him..." I stopped myself, realizing what Chuck's father must be going through. He had to go to bed each night, not knowing if his son was dead or alive.

"We're all waiting for him," he added. "At least waiting for word on where he is."

My eyes filled with tears as I imagined all kinds of awful scenarios, none of which I wanted Jeannie to consider. Chuck's dad turned away and stifled what sounded like a sniffle. He was clearly uncomfortable expressing emotion around a stranger.

"If I hear anything, I'll let you know," he said, clearing his throat. "What's the best way to contact you?"

I gave him Jim's name and the phone number to the apartment complex. I was in a daze as I walked back to the car. Jim jumped out when he saw me coming.

"Are you okay?" he asked. "What happened?"

I climbed in and told him everything. Tears spilled, and Jim took me in his arms and held me tight. He rubbed my back and tried to soothe me.

"Poor Jeannie," he said.

We drove to my house in silence.

Jim parked but kept the engine running. "Do you want me to tell her?" he offered, trying to save me from the dreaded task.

I considered us going in together, both of us telling her, but decided against it. "It's best if I do it," I said.

"I understand." He squeezed my hand, and I gave him a kiss before getting out of the car.

"Good luck," he said. "Let's go out to dinner tomorrow night. Bring Jeannie along if she's up for it."

I smiled at him. "Okay."

Jim drove away. Then I heard the front door open and saw Jeannie.

"What did you find out?" she asked.

It had gotten dark outside, so she couldn't see me until I got closer. Then, when she could make out my face, she repeated, "What did you find out, Lou?" Her shaky voice meant she could tell by my expression that it wasn't good.

"Why don't you put your coat on, and we'll go for a walk," I said.

Jeannie disappeared and returned wearing her coat, gloves, and scarf. Then she followed me outside. I had planned to go to the park and tell her there, but she grabbed my arm and said, "I want to know what you found out about Chuck."

I stopped and looked at her. "He's missing," I said. "They don't know where he is."

Jeannie looked confused, like it wasn't something she'd

considered. "Like he took off?" she asked. "Went AWOL?"

"No. He's missing in action."

She looked at me, horrified. "No!"

She wobbled a bit, so I grabbed hold of her, worried she may faint. As I pulled her close, she kept shouting, "No," over and over. Eventually, the shouts faded to sobs, and all I was able to do was hold her in my arms and pray to God that what we were both thinking wasn't true.

Chapter 18

As the school year went on, Jeannie's grades got progressively worse. She wasn't into studying that much to begin with, and with the added stress of worrying about Chuck, her mind just wasn't there.

"You've got to get her to focus," Bernice warned as we finished cleaning one of the units so the tenants could move in.

"I've tried. She's just too preoccupied. The only time I've seen her in a decent mood was when I asked her to help me decide on furniture." I put the last of the cleaning supplies in the bucket and gathered our things. "I wish Chuck's dad would hear some news soon. I mean, if Chuck is dead, she could at least grieve him and move on. It's this being in limbo thing that's got her so down."

Bernice didn't seem to fully understand. Studying came first with her, no matter what. She'd never let a boy come between her and her books.

"How about we talk about a happier topic," she suggested. "Like your wedding and eighteenth birthday."

I grinned. "Only a few more weeks. Jim's already got the apartment set up. We're just waiting on the stove to be delivered."

"Pretty soon you'll be a married woman. We won't be able to get into trouble like we used to."

I burst out laughing. "What do you mean? We've never gotten into trouble. We're the dullest kids around."

"I had an overdue library book once," Bernice joked, and the look on her face made me laugh even harder.

We locked the apartment.

"Well, we've got three more weeks to get crazy. This is our last chance," Bernice declared.

"You want to pitch pennies at the old spot? See if we can

score some gum?" I suggested, feeling a little nostalgic.

"I got a better idea. How about we go to Marshall Field's and get a dress for me to wear to the wedding?"

"Okay. You want to eat at the Walnut Room afterward?"

"Yes!" Bernice said.

If that was our version of getting crazy, it was fine by me.

We dropped the buckets and cleaning supplies off at my house, then walked to Bernice's so she could get some money. After a brief train ride, we arrived under the big green State Street clock and went inside.

The evening gowns were beautiful but a bit too glamorous for our wedding, a small ceremony conducted by a justice of the peace. "Look at these," Bernice said as she pointed at a section of day dresses that were more appropriate. We browsed and chose a few, and then a saleslady offered to take us to a fitting room. Bernice spun around after trying on each one, and after hemming and hawing, we chose a floral number that went well with shoes she already owned.

With that taken care of, Bernice and I headed to the Walnut Room, where a serious-looking older gentleman greeted us and took us to our table. Once seated, I glanced around, admiring the walnut-paneled walls, Austrian chandeliers, and opulent marble fountain.

"Everything looks so good," Bernice said as she eyed the menu. "But I have to get the chicken pot pie since it's all everyone talks about."

"Me, too," I said, hungry from cleaning and shopping all day.

The waiter took our order, two pot pies and two Cokes, and then disappeared.

"You getting nervous about the big night yet?" Bernice asked.

I paused. Like most girls, I had planned on waiting until my wedding night. The waiter returned and set our Cokes on the table. Bernice reached for hers and took a sip.

"We already did it," I said.

Bernice's eyes bulged, and she almost choked on her drink. "And you didn't tell me?"

"I was worried you'd think I was a floozy."

She looked me in the eye. "I would never think that about you." Then she leaned in and whispered, "I heard it hurts."

"It only hurts the first time."

Bernice smiled. "The first time? How many times did you do it? Wait...don't answer that." She sighed. "I've never even kissed a guy yet."

"Well, it's not like you didn't have opportunities. You put the kibosh on every one," I reminded her.

"True."

Our food came and the scent rising from the flaky crust was heavenly. I poked the pie with my fork, blew on it and took a bite.

"Mmm," I said. "This is almost as good as sex."

Bernice's eyes grew large again, then she snorted, and we laughed between bites of the most amazing pot pies we'd ever tasted.

The next few weeks flew by. Mom and Dad were preparing for me to get married and leave home, which seemed to both excite and depress them, and I was studying for exams, packing my belongings, and trying to cheer up Jeannie.

"Once school's out, I'm going to need a lot of help unpacking," I told her.

"No problem," she said.

"And next weekend, the sofa is being delivered. Jim has an appointment across town, and I don't want to be alone when the delivery men show up. Do you think you can stay with me?"

Jeannie looked at me. "Sure."

She was a girl of few words nowadays, but at least she was talking. Mom and Dad had grown increasingly worried about her as time went on, and my story of "she's just at that age" was becoming less and less believable.

"We're having dinner after the wedding at Mariano's," Mom said as we folded laundry. "I figured since we're a small group, that would be the perfect place."

Mom and Dad had insisted on paying for the food. Jim's dad fought them on it but gave in when they said they wouldn't hear of him treating. The truth was Jim's dad could have paid for a lavish reception, but he and Jim decided that would be a waste of money and that it was better to invest in expanding their business.

I didn't care much about the reception. All I could think about was that I was getting married. It was a day I had dreamt of since I was a little girl. I smiled to myself, remembering my western dream again. Jim was no rancher, but he made me happier than anyone else, and I knew he would make a great father, one who could provide for his family.

On the last day of school, Bernice and I were getting ready to walk home when Frankie came over.

"Hey, Lou. I heard you and Jim are engaged. I just wanted to say congratulations. Jim's a great guy."

"Thanks," I replied, letting bygones be bygones. "I think so, too."

He nodded and moved along, then Bernice and I went to her house.

"I've got a surprise for you," she said when we walked into her room.

"You do?"

She reached into her top dresser drawer and pulled out a bag from Marshall Field's. I had been with her the whole time and hadn't seen her buy anything other than the dress.

"How'd you—?"

"My mom and I went back together." She smiled and handed it to me. "Open it. It's an early birthday present/wedding gift."

I set the bag down, pulled the tissue-wrapped contents out, and carefully opened the spot that had been secured with a sticker. It was one of the most exquisite ivory lace and silk nightgowns I'd ever seen.

I lifted it by its straps and admired it. "It's beautiful," I said. "I can't believe you did this. I love it!"

Bernice smiled. "Good," she said. "Seeing you happy made those few extra nights of babysitting worth it."

I knew how she loathed watching the twins next door, preferring to work at the apartment complex for Jim's dad. That made the gift extra special.

"Thanks so much. This means a lot to me."

She nodded. "You're welcome. Only the best for my best friend."

We went outside afterward. I pulled a penny out of my pocket and threw it against the side of the house. I watched as it landed in the grass instead of on the cement below. "I'm pretty rusty," I said.

Bernice walked over and collected the coin. She blew the dust off it, then stepped back, got into position, and tossed. The penny sailed through the air, tapped the side of the house, and fell straight down, landing where the first brick met the pavement.

She turned to me and smiled. "I still got it."

"Yes, you do."

We took turns throwing the penny until the sun began to set, painting the sky burnt orange. Then, when we couldn't see what we were doing anymore, we called it a night. I thanked her for the gift again and began walking home. With every step, it felt like I was saying goodbye to my childhood.

Chapter 19

The big day had finally arrived. I was so excited that I jumped from my bed and dashed to the kitchen. Dad was sitting at the table drinking a cup of coffee, and Mom and Jeannie were cooking eggs and bacon.

"Happy Birthday," Jeannie said when she saw me come in.

"Happy Birthday," my parents echoed, smiling.

Mom handed me a plate of food and a glass of orange juice. "We thought it would be nice to make you breakfast on your wedding day," she said.

"Thanks, you guys." I sat down.

Dad glanced my way. "Before you know it, we'll be coming over to eat at *your* house," he said.

I smiled but felt a little sad. It would be weird not seeing him, Mom, and Jeannie every day. "I'll have everyone over for dinner as soon as we're settled in." I was already missing them.

When we finished eating, Mom turned to me. "Your father and I already showered, and Jeannie is going to clean up next. Then everyone is out of your way, and you can take your time getting ready."

"Thanks," I said. Between Mom and Jeannie and Bernice, I didn't have a care in the world. All I had to do was focus on being a happy bride.

Jeannie hopped from her chair and headed to the bathroom, then Dad rose and went to the couch while Mom cleared the table. I tried to help her, but she shooed me away, so I went to lie down and relax.

The room seemed so bare now that most of my things had been packed and were at the apartment. All that was left was the bed, the dresser, and the drapes. Mom said they were going to use it as a guest bedroom now.

As I rested, my mind drifted to Jim. I began thinking about

what he would do to me tonight, and my heart started beating faster. We would get to sleep next to each other too and be able to every night for the rest of our lives.

The idea made me so happy. As I lay there smiling, I heard a knock on the door.

"Hey, Mom," I said as she came and sat next to me.

She had a rectangular wooden box in her hand. "I've got something for you." She lifted the lid. Inside was a vintage silver necklace with pale blue stones. "It was Aunt Violet's. I thought you might want to borrow it so you have something blue."

I carefully lifted it off the faded black velvet, went to the mirror, and held it against my neck. "It's so beautiful. It'll be perfect with the dress."

"Now you've got something borrowed and something blue," she said.

"True," I said as I turned back to her. "Thanks, Mom."

She smiled and patted my knee. "I'll let you rest until Jeannie's done." Then she got up and left, closing the door behind her. I closed my eyes, happy that I had jewelry to wear with my dress. And not just any old jewelry, an estate piece from Aunt Violet.

When Jeannie was done, I got in the tub and shaved my legs. I soaked in the bubbles and didn't rush, which felt nice. Then I moisturized my skin and styled my hair, pinning it into place the way I'd practiced beforehand so it would look elegant.

I applied light makeup and put on Aunt Violet's necklace, making sure the clasp was secure. Once I'd gotten dressed and slipped on my shoes, I stepped into the family room.

"Whoa," Jeannie said. "You look pretty."

"Stunning," Dad added.

"Thanks," I said, feeling slightly embarrassed.

Mom stood at his side, beaming. Her face was so filled with emotion all she could do was nod in agreement.

I nodded back, letting her know I understood her

predicament. "Guess I'm all set then."

We drove to the courthouse and met Jim, his dad, and Bernice. I had asked Jim if his mom would be coming in from New York, and he said he hadn't invited her, so I let it drop. Since the divorce, they hadn't been close, and I didn't want to push the issue. Also, he hadn't made any close friends since moving to Chicago, none he felt should be included in our celebration, so the event was a lot more intimate.

Jim's dad led the way to the room where the ceremony was going to be held.

The justice of the peace was a wiry older man who saw us coming and waved. "Welcome. Welcome."

He reviewed our paperwork and asked us if we were ready to get started. And when we nodded yes, he began.

I recited the lines he asked me to repeat, and as I did, everyone faded away except Jim. In no time, the man was saying, "You may kiss the bride." And then Jim pressed his lips gently against mine, making me his wife.

The spell was broken by the sound of clapping. Our little group might have been small, but they sure knew how to make a lot of noise. Jim's dad shook Jim's hand, and then, before any of us could start crying, he pulled out his new Kodak camera and said, "Let me take a few pictures."

Jim and I posed together for several shots. Then he took some of the family. The justice of the peace was kind enough to take one of the entire group. We were about to leave when Bernice asked Jim's dad, "Will you take one of just the two of us?"

"Sure," he said, lifting the camera.

Bernice and I stood side by side. Instead of standing up straight and matching our pose to our attire and circumstances, we threw our arms around each other's shoulders and slouched while grinning ear to ear.

Mom and Dad congratulated Jim and me, and then Jim's dad gave me a hug, something he'd never done before. He'd always seemed quiet and reserved, which Jim promised would change once he got to know me better.

Jeannie put out her hand so I could slap it, so I smiled and slapped hers back.

"Who's ready to eat?" Dad asked.

A chorus of "I am's" filled the air.

Jim had decorated his car with a sign that read *Just Married* and had affixed streams of colored ribbon to his bumper instead of cans so he didn't chance chipping the paint. On the way to the restaurant, strangers honked and waved at us, so we smiled and waved back, enjoying the extra attention on our special day.

A heavyset Italian man with a booming voice greeted us and showed us to our table, a round one with a white tablecloth and a three-wick candle in the center surrounded by rose petals. Everyone took a seat, and the waiter appeared with champagne and poured us each a glass.

"To Jim and Lou," Dad toasted. "May they live a long and happy life together."

Jim smiled at me and gave me a peck on the lips. We clinked glasses with everyone and took a sip of bubbly. Shortly afterward, the food arrived: a big bowl of salad, grilled chicken, and lasagna. Everything tasted like ambrosia, but I didn't want to overeat and get a tummy ache, so I ate until I was comfortably full and saved room for cake.

Everyone chatted as we ate, sharing stories from the past.

"...and then there was the time Jim beat up a mugger who was trying to steal an old lady's purse in Central Park," Jim's dad said.

I glanced at Jim. He shrugged like it was no big deal.

Jeannie started giggling. "How about that time you got in trouble when we went to visit Aunt Violet?" she said, looking my way.

Bernice shot me a look, and I made eye contact with Mom. She smiled, clearly over it.

"You know how it is when you're a kid," Mom said. "You say whatever is on your mind without thinking." She shared the infamous old folks' home story, eliciting howls of laughter all around. I laughed, too, realizing I'd never live it down no matter how much time passed.

A little while later, Jim reached for my hand and held my gaze. I knew what was on his mind because it was the same thing that had been on mine all day.

When we'd finished our cake, the waiter wrapped a bunch of leftovers for us and put them in a bag. "In case you're hungry later," he said, winking.

We said goodbye to everyone and drove to our new place, a two-bedroom unit in the apartment complex Jim helped manage for his dad. He unlocked the door, scooped me up, and carried me to the bedroom. I kicked my shoes off as he set me on the bed and kissed me passionately.

He pulled away and said, "I just remembered I bought candles. Let me go get them."

After he left, I slipped out of my wedding dress and into the nightgown Bernice had given me. Wearing it made me feel glamorous, like a movie star. Jim returned with the candles, and his jaw dropped.

"God...you look so beautiful," he said.

He set the lit candles on the dresser and turned off the light. Instead of rushing to me, he stayed where he was, admiring me from afar. Even though we'd already done it a few times, my heart pounded hard in my chest. I could barely breathe when he placed his hands on the straps of the gown and slid them over my shoulders.

I stood before him, completely naked, and looked into his eyes.

"I love you, Louise. I'm so happy you're my wife," he said. He undressed quickly and carried me to the bed.

An hour later, I was spent. I had been beating myself up over sleeping with him before our wedding night, thinking how upset I would be if Jeannie had pulled a stunt like that, but as I lay next to him, I was elated. This was the best it had been yet, and he promised that it would only get better. We would have a lifetime to discover just how good we could be together.

Chapter 20

The next few weeks were blissful. I spent my days unpacking boxes and my nights snuggling up to Jim. Once the apartment was set up, we had everyone over for a dinner party, which went off without a hitch, and afterward, the place finally felt like home.

Jim and I settled into a comfortable pattern, and soon after, I found myself worrying about Jeannie again. I knew she was still hurting; there was still no word on Chuck, and she had hinted she might not return to school in the fall, that she might get a job instead.

"I think you should finish school," I told her. "I don't see why you want to give up."

Jeannie sighed, clearly frustrated I was siding with Mom and Dad on this. "I'm not giving up," she said. "I'm just not interested in studying anymore. I'd rather get a job and earn money."

We went back and forth for an hour, and I thought I'd made some good points. But a week later, Mom called and told me Jeannie had started working at a factory, sewing lace onto garments. She used to value my advice, but it had fallen on deaf ears this time.

"How's the new job?" I asked the next time I was over, deciding not to hassle her about her decision.

"It's good," she said.

We chatted for a while about her new position, and I pulled her aside. "I was thinking about Chuck's dad, thinking maybe he lost Jim's number and doesn't know how to reach me. You think we should go over there and check on things?"

"Yeah," she said. "Let's go over there. Why didn't I think of that?"

I knew why, because she was depressed. I thought she wouldn't want to meet Chuck's dad since her and Chuck's relationship had been a secret, but she seemed past caring about that now. She needed news – good or bad – so she could finally find some peace.

We decided to go that weekend.

On the bus ride over, Jeannie's face was drawn.

"You okay?" I asked.

"Yeah. I'm just worried about what he might say."

I reached for her hand and squeezed it. I was worried, too, because if Chuck had returned and hadn't contacted her, she'd be hurt. If he'd been killed, she'd be hurt more. None of the outcomes seemed good, but knowing was still better than not knowing.

The hot summer air was thick with humidity as we stepped off the bus, adding more discomfort to the long walk to the house. Once we arrived, I climbed the stairs and turned to Jeannie. She nodded.

I rang the bell, and a moment later, Chuck's dad opened the door, looking much older than the last time I'd seen him.

"Nice to see you," he said, looking at my sister. "You must be Jeannie."

"How'd you know?" she asked.

Chuck's dad smiled. "You two look alike." He let out a deep breath. "I wish I had news for you ladies. I really do. But they still don't know where he is." He shook his head. "Makes no damn sense."

We were back to square one. "Well, we just thought we'd stop by in case you might have heard anything," I said.

"I understand. You'll be the first to know when I get news. I've still got your number," he said as if reading my mind. He turned to Jeannie. "I can see why he likes you. You're a beautiful girl."

Jeannie's cheeks turned pink as she flushed with embarrassment. "Thank you," she mumbled.

We said our goodbyes and headed to the bus stop. On the way there, Jeannie turned to me. "Do you mind if we just walk?"

The apartment was several miles away, and even though I wasn't keen on making the trip in the muggy heat, I said okay. Maybe the jaunt would dispel some of her frustration.

We strolled in silence, the occasional car passing by the only sound keeping us company. After we'd gone several blocks, Jeannie burst into tears.

"I can't take this anymore," she sobbed.

I rubbed her back. "I know." I didn't know what to say. All I knew was matters of the heart couldn't be rushed.

By the time we got back to my place, Jeannie was exhausted. I offered her some dinner, but she refused, asking if Jim could give her a ride home instead. He did, and when he returned, he frowned and said, "Such a sad situation. I wish she could get over him, but I could see how it would be hard to do not knowing his whereabouts." He dug into his meal, and as we cuddled on the sofa afterward, I thanked God for the life I had and prayed Jeannie's would get better soon.

Later that night, I woke up drenched in sweat, my neck muscles tense.

"You okay?" Jim asked in a soft voice.

I sat up. "Yeah. Just a bad dream."

"You wanna talk about it?"

I glanced at him. "Only if you've got time for a long story."

Jim propped his elbow on his pillow and leaned his head on his hand. "I've always got time for you," he said.

I told him the story of the Williams family and how I used to have the recurring dream about trying to save them.

"I haven't had that one in a long time," I said.

Jim caressed the side of my face. "Maybe it was stress that brought it on."

"You're probably right."

He pulled me close and wrapped his arms around me, and

within minutes I drifted into a peaceful slumber.

***

When senior year started, I thought it would feel weird to be married and in high school at the same time. But oddly enough, it turned out to be a boon to my popularity. Other girls wanted to sit with me and chat, which made time fly and classes much more enjoyable.

"They hope some of your good luck will rub off on them," Bernice said. When they weren't around, she called them *Lou's entourage*.

"How come I don't have an entourage?" she asked as we did our math homework.

"Because you're antisocial," I reminded her.

"Oh yeah." She looked unconcerned and pulled a pencil from behind her ear to erase a mistake she had made. She sat up straight and glanced at me. "So Jeannie's not coming back to school, huh?"

"No." I sighed. "She likes her new job, and making money seems to have lifted her spirits, so I don't think she'll be back. Plus, she met a guy at work."

Bernice raised an eyebrow. "A guy? Well, that part sounds positive. Maybe he can take her mind off Chuck."

"I think that's why she started seeing him." I set my book aside. "He's really nice and good-looking, but Jeannie said being around him isn't like being around Chuck."

"Poor Jeannie. Maybe in time she'll like him more, or she'll find someone better."

I shrugged. "I hope so."

The remainder of the school year flew by. Things were great with Jim, but he was swamped working with his dad, trying to expand the business, so I used my free time hanging out with Bernice, Jeannie, and her new boyfriend, Tad.

Tad had turned out to be a great guy. Jim liked him, I liked him, my parents liked him, and thankfully, Jeannie was starting to like him for who he was rather than comparing him to someone else.

Life was good, but I was a bundle of emotions on graduation day. I was happy I had finished school, worried I hadn't gotten pregnant yet even though Jim and I were trying every night, and sad that Bernice was going to New Mexico.

I sighed, trying not to let myself feel down on such an important day, then remembered someone had said Frankie signed up to fight in Vietnam.

"I heard you're leaving," I said after I found him.

"Yeah," he said. "I want to make a difference and serve my country."

There were a lot of conflicting opinions about the war, but Frankie seemed confident in his decision.

"I'm sure you will make us proud," I told him, looking him in the eyes.

"Thanks, Lou. I really appreciate you saying that."

I extended a hand. He reached out and shook it. "Take care, Frank."

"You, too."

Saying goodbye to Frank was easy. Bernice leaving for college was hard.

Her parents pulled up in front of the apartment building. The car was all packed, and Bernice got out.

"Time to go," she said. She wore a brave face but looked on the verge of tears.

"You're coming back to visit, right?" I asked.

"Yep. Spending summers at home."

"Good," I replied, my voice cracking.

Bernice gave me a hug. She squeezed me so tight it felt like my ribs were being crushed. When she finally let go, I smiled at her.

"I expect straight A's," I said.

"I'll do my best," she said, smiling back.

I watched as she climbed into the backseat of her parents' car, and they drove away. When they were gone, my eyes were filled with tears. I wanted to be happy for Bernice. I really did.

It was just hard to say goodbye to my best friend.

Chapter 21

The rest of summer, Jim and his dad kept me busy with a bunch of projects. I planted perennials that attracted new renters. They included me in their business brainstorming sessions, saying they needed a female perspective to better understand their customer base's wants and needs. I'd also offered myself up as a babysitter on Thursday nights after discovering some of the moms in the building were looking for a night out, and before I knew it, my Thursday evenings were booked until the end of the year.

"I want to get a second building," Jim's dad said as he took a bite of his lunch. "And I want people to think of renting with us before anyone else." He set his fork down. "What do you think we can do to stand out from the competition?"

My mind drew a blank as I stared at my salad.

"How about we offer a free gift when they sign a lease? Like a toaster or a radio," Jim suggested.

"Wouldn't that be too expensive?" I asked. I wasn't sure how we would be able to do that and still make money.

"Nope. We'll just roll it into the cost of the rent," Jim said.

"Oh." I smiled at him. He was not only handsome but smart.

Later that night, Bernice called. "I'm nervous about starting school tomorrow."

"Don't worry. You'll do great," I told her. I took a sip of Coke. "So what have you been up to? Did you have fun with your parents?"

"Yeah, we had a lot of fun. My aunt took us to El Santuario de Chimayo. It's this old adobe church that's known for miraculous healing. People with serious illnesses claim to have been cured by rubbing the holy dirt on themselves."

"Wow! That's pretty neat."

"Yeah, it was. After that, we went horseback riding, did some shopping. Oh, and we went to Juan's house for dinner. His parents threw a big party for Alejandro's birthday."

"I thought Alejandro moved to Arizona?"

"He did, but he came back. He said it was too hot all the time, and he missed the four seasons in Santa Fe."

Her voice sounded bubblier than usual. "*And?*" I asked.

"And he's as handsome as ever," she exclaimed. "I sat across from him at dinner and couldn't stop staring at him the whole time."

I grinned, remembering how adamant she had been about not getting involved with anyone before school, saying the focus was on studying. "So, did he pay any attention to you this time?"

"Yeah. He was really nice to me. He spent a lot of time talking to me, asking me about school, about Chicago."

"So, did you get the feeling he likes you, or do you think he was just being polite?"

There was silence, then she said, "We kissed."

"What?" I shrieked. I glanced back at Jim, who was sitting on the sofa, shaking his head and smiling.

"I know. I've been dying to tell you the story," Bernice said in a hushed tone. "After dinner, we went for a walk and talked, like I told you. He seemed genuinely interested in everything I had to say and told me he admired my spirit for following my dream of getting a business degree. Then he told me he had planned to go to college too but had been in a bad relationship and suffered a broken heart, so he took a job in Arizona to get away from it all."

"So why did he come back?"

"He tells people he returned for the weather, but he told me he came back because New Mexico is his home, and it's not worth losing time with his family because of a girl. He also smiled at me and said, 'Besides, there are much better girls to choose from anyway.'"

I was so excited I almost shrieked again. "Is that when he kissed you?"

"No. It was later. When we came back from our walk, my parents were still there. They had been reluctant to let us go on our own until he said it was just around the property. They looked a little anxious, but I think they're just nervous about leaving me to fend for myself in another state."

"But you're not fending for yourself. You have your aunt, your friend Juan, and *Alejandro*." I said.

Bernice laughed. "I think he's what they're most afraid of."

I didn't care what her parents feared; I wanted to hear the juicy parts. "So when did he kiss you?"

"I'm getting to that," she assured me. "So when we got back, Juan called me away to help with dishes. He told me they were going to hang out later and asked if I wanted to come, so I said yes. After we went back to my aunt's and my parents went to bed, I snuck out to meet Juan and Alejandro as planned."

"You snuck out?" I found it hard to believe.

"And drank tequila," she added.

"No way!"

"I know. It doesn't sound like me, right?"

"No." It was unreal. Only a short time out west and Bernice had turned lawless.

"The three of us met in the barn and shared some of Alejandro's dad's tequila, the good kind, he said, and after we got to talking, Juan said he was tired and went to bed. Then it was just Alejandro and me."

Finally, the good part, I thought.

"I was feeling a little tipsy and ended up telling him I had a crush on him when I visited last time. He smiled and said I was just a girl before, but I had grown up and become a beautiful woman. Then he kissed me."

"That's so romantic! Then what happened?"

"We kissed for a while longer, and then he said I'd better go home before my parents woke up and found me gone. He said he didn't want to get on their bad side." Bernice laughed. "Luckily, I managed to sneak in undetected, and since my parents went home, I've been spending all my free time with him."

"So he's your boyfriend."

"We haven't had the talk yet, but yes."

"Oh my gosh! This is great news. I'm so happy for you." I paused. "So…has anything else happened?"

"We haven't done *that*." She paused and added, "But I'm finding it really hard to say no."

For a girl who had always been in control, that came as a surprise. Then again, maybe she'd grown tired of being so rigid.

"You'll know when the time is right," I said.

"It feels like the time is right every time he's nearby."

I giggled, completely understanding where she was coming from.

"Well, I should probably get going," she said. "First day and all tomorrow."

"Good luck. And don't worry. You'll do great."

"I hope so. I heard college is a lot harder than high school."

"Yeah. Maybe you'll get a B in something. The horror," I joked.

Bernice laughed. "That would be awful." She sighed and asked, "How's Jeannie been?"

"She's good. She just got a promotion at work, and Tad is planning to go to school to become a journalist. She finally seems happy."

"Glad to hear it. Make sure to tell her I said hello."

"I will."

We wrapped up our conversation, and after I hung up the phone, it rang again. I answered on the first ring, thinking Bernice had forgotten to say something. Instead, a man's voice said, "Hi, Lou. It's Chuck."

Chapter 22

When we finished talking, Jim rose from the sofa. "Is everything okay?" he asked. "You look upset."

"I'm not upset. I'm in shock."

"Why? What's going on?"

"That was Chuck," I said, my voice shaky.

"You mean missing-in-Vietnam Chuck?"

"Yeah. Looking for Jeannie."

It took a moment for what I said to sink in.

"Oh man," he said, rubbing his face.

"I know." I took a seat at the kitchen table. "I don't know what to do. Jeannie seems so happy with Tad, and now this happens, but I've got to tell her, right?"

"You've got to," Jim reiterated as he sat down opposite me.

The thought of calling Jeannie made my stomach lurch. I didn't know if I should be happy for her or if I should be concerned. All I knew was I didn't want to see her hurt.

I pictured telling Jeannie over the phone and her freaking out, causing our parents to ask a bunch of questions. We didn't need that kind of drama. We managed to keep them in the dark so far, and we couldn't blow it now.

"Will you give me a ride to my parents' house?" I asked Jim. "I want to talk to her in person."

"Of course," he said, getting up.

As Jim drove, my stomach tightened into a knot. This was the good news we had been hoping to hear all along, and I should have been elated, not feeling like I was going to be ill.

Jeannie answered, wearing a big smile. "Hey, what are you doing here?" she asked.

"I came to talk to you. You want to go for a drive?"

"I can't right now. Tad's over, and we just finished dinner."

"Shit," I said.

"Why? What's going on?" Jeannie asked, looking concerned.

"I can't talk now. But come by afterward, and if possible, bring stuff to stay overnight."

"Okay," she said, eyeing me like I was a crazy woman. "Do you want to come in and at least say hello?"

"Not tonight," I said, walking away. "See you later."

As we drove off, I realized my rude behavior must have seemed odd, but the truth was I didn't want to face Tad. I was already feeling uncomfortable, and seeing him would only make what I had to do harder.

When I got home, I paced the apartment until the doorbell rang an hour later.

"What's going on?" Jeannie asked as she came in.

I offered her a chair, and I sat down too.

"I got a phone call from Chuck," I said in a soft voice.

All the color drained from Jeannie's face. "You mean…he's alive?"

"Yes. And he asked for you." I pulled a piece of paper from my pocket and handed it to her. "I took down his number and told him you'd call him back."

She took it from me, wordlessly staring at the number while I held my breath, hoping the news would make her happy. Instead, she burst into tears.

"This can't be happening," she sobbed. "Not now."

I knew it. Total disaster. "I didn't want to tell you because I know you've moved on, but I thought you'd want to know."

Jeannie kept crying. I pulled my chair next to hers and rubbed her back. "It's too late," was all she said.

"It's not too late," I assured her. "Chuck's alive, and you still have a chance if you want him."

Jeannie lifted her tear-soaked face and said, "I'm pregnant, Lou. I just found out. And I know Tad wants to marry me."

I sat staring at my sister, speechless.

"Oh my God," I whispered. She nodded and broke into another wave of tears. Comprehension sunk in as my mind worked to find a solution. "Do you love him?"

Jeannie's forehead crinkled. "He's a nice person, Lou. I love him, but not the way I love Chuck."

I steeled myself before saying what I had been quietly pondering ever since Jeannie met Tad. "Have you ever considered that your love for Chuck was just a schoolgirl crush? I mean, I understand it – of course, I do. But you hardly knew him..."

"Why would you say such a thing?"

"I just...no, you're right. I'm sorry. It was a stupid thing to say. But it would be so much easier if you could just let him go."

"I can't, Lou."

"Does Tad know you're pregnant?"

She wiped her eyes with the back of her hand. "No. I haven't told him yet."

I tapped my fingers on the kitchen table. "Okay. I'm not sure if this is good advice, but it's what I would do, right or wrong."

Jeannie listened closely.

"Call Chuck back. Then go see him right away. I mean, you never know. You may be in love with a memory. You may see him again and not feel the same."

Jeannie looked anxious. "But what if I do feel the same? Then it will hurt even more because I can't have him."

"Well, you're going to have to face him sooner or later. And the sooner you do it and find out how you feel, the better. For your health," I said, pointing at her abdomen.

Jeannie rubbed her face. She rose and said, "I need to use the restroom." She hurried off, and when she returned ten minutes later, she looked like she had washed her face and fixed her hair.

She took a few deep breaths, unfolded the paper, and reached for the phone. I went into the next room, not wanting to crowd her. Jim had gone to his dad's in an attempt to give us some privacy. His dad had seemed a little lonely lately, and he offered to take him out for a drink. I wasn't sure if that was true or if he was just giving us space. But the way things were going, I almost wished I was at the bar with them.

"I never thought I'd see you again," I heard Jeannie say. "But I never stopped hoping." There was silence on her end, then, "I missed you, too. So much. Okay. See you soon," she said, sounding excited, and she hung up.

I came back into the kitchen, and Jeannie turned to me. "He's coming to pick me up."

I let out a breath I'd been holding. "I hope this is the right thing to do. Well, at least you'll know, and then you'll be able to make a decision."

"What do you mean?" Jeannie asked.

I locked eyes with her. "If you decide you want Chuck, you'll have to tell him about your current condition. Then he has to decide what he wants to do. If he wants to move forward together, you can choose him. If he doesn't..."

Jeannie was quiet for a moment. "So you're saying if he wants to move forward, I don't tell Tad about the baby?"

"I probably will regret saying this, but...yeah. You don't tell anyone except Chuck and me. And I won't tell anyone."

"Even Jim?" she asked.

"No. This secret would stay with us."

Jeannie thought it over, then flung her arms around me. "Thank you, Lou," she said, squeezing me tight.

I held her in my arms, hating that I'd thought up such a morally reprehensible plan. But my kid sister's future hung in the balance, and if doing something shameful meant Jeannie might have a shot at a happy life instead of living one devoid of passion, I'd live with the guilt.

"I'm not sure what time I'll be back. Is that okay?"

"It's fine," I said. "Mom and Dad know you're staying over, so nothing to worry about there, and I'll sleep on the sofa so I can hear you knock. I don't want to wake Jim."

"Okay," she said, smiling. "Thanks again."

"Don't thank me. I didn't do anything."

She fidgeted with her hair while staring out the window. Suddenly she gasped. "He's here," she said. "I'm going to meet him outside."

"Good luck," I said.

I peeked through the curtains as Chuck got out of his car and slowly approached Jeannie. They talked for a few minutes, and he took her in his arms, spinning her around. I heard her laughing, and a minute later, they hopped in the car and drove off into the night.

While Jeannie was gone, I tried to read a romance novel I'd just bought, but after a half-hour, I set it aside. I couldn't focus. All I could do was wonder how their meeting was going while second-guessing my advice. I washed and dried the dishes, hoping things were going well, and soon afterward, Jim came home from drinks with his dad.

I explained that Jeannie had gone to meet Chuck.

"The plot thickens," he said, kissing me on the cheek. His breath smelled of alcohol, but he wasn't drunk. "How about we fool around before she comes back? It will help you relax."

I followed him to the bedroom, and we made love. Once he'd fallen asleep, I went to the sofa where I lay wide awake. A sliver of moonlight shone through the half-open drapes, acting as a nightlight while I worried and waited for Jeannie to return.

Chapter 23

I woke early the next morning and noticed Jeannie hadn't come home yet. During breakfast, Jim told me not to worry, that he was sure she'd come over or call soon. I didn't know how he managed to stay calm when things were so up in the air, and after he left for work, I got really nervous, letting my mind construct all kinds of awful scenarios.

An hour later, I heard a light knock on the door. I ran to answer it, and thankfully, it was Jeannie. "I thought you had gotten into an accident. I was worried."

"Sorry," Jeannie replied. "We stayed up all night talking, so I decided to stay over. I was going to call, but by the time I thought of it, I assumed you'd already be asleep."

"You're right. Plus, it would have woke Jim, and he's got to work. So how did it go? Wait. Before you get started, you want some breakfast?"

"God. That would be great. I'm starved."

Jeannie and I headed to the kitchen, and she sat down as I grabbed some eggs, bread, and orange juice out of the refrigerator.

"So, where has he been all this time?" I asked as I broke two eggs into a bowl.

"He was taken captive in Vietnam. Somehow, he got split up from his platoon and got lost in the jungle. The next thing he knew, he woke up in a small room with a mud floor and a splitting headache. He said he must have been butted with the back of a gun."

"Oh my God! That's awful!" I said as I poured the eggs into the frying pan.

"I know. He's lucky to be alive." She was getting emotional just telling me, so I didn't press for details. "Eventually, he managed to escape, and he's home now, safe and sound, although traumatized."

I began buttering her toast. "He didn't say what happened while he was there, did he?"

Jeannie pursed her lips. "He said he didn't want to talk about that."

I nodded, handing her the plate of food. "So, what did you decide after you spent the night talking?"

"I choose him." Jeannie smiled, but it was a tired smile.

"Poor Tad. I mean...I'm happy for you, but..." I sighed. "How did the conversation about the baby go?"

Jeannie looked down. "I didn't tell him."

"What do you mean you didn't tell him?"

Jeannie took a drink of orange juice. "I found another way."

"What way? Wait...you're not thinking of getting rid of the baby?"

"Chuck wants to marry me," she replied. "He said we've lost enough time, and he knows I'm the one."

"But won't he be able to put two and two together and do the math?"

"There's no math," Jeannie stated. "He asked me to marry him, and I said yes. Then he asked if we could sleep together, and I said we could, but only if we get married right away."

My jaw hung open. "You mean?"

"Yep."

"And then he'll think..." I whispered.

"Yep."

"How far along are you?"

"Not far. Look, Lou. It's going to work. It has to."

"This could come back to haunt you later."

I sat in silence, my stomach in knots. As if my dishonest plan wasn't bad enough, now it had expanded and meant lying to another person.

I got up to get a glass of water.

"But I want Chuck. What else could I have done?" Jeannie asked, searching my face for answers.

I turned on the faucet, filled my glass, and turned to face her. "You could have told him. If he really loved you, he'd be okay with everything. Maybe he would. Oh, I don't know, Jeannie. But what's done is done, I guess."

"You think I should have told him?"

I gave her question serious thought before answering. "I think in a perfect world, you wouldn't be put in such a crappy position. Chuck wouldn't have been captured, and you never would have dated Tad." Jeannie stared at me, waiting for a straight answer. "I think you followed your heart and did what you felt was right. I'll keep my part of the bargain. The secret stays with us."

Jeannie exhaled. It looked like a weight had been lifted from her shoulders.

"So it was better with Chuck?" I asked, trying to lighten the mood.

Jeannie blushed. "A million times better."

"Well, at least there's that." I grinned, and as I did, a thought occurred to me. "How are you going to get married when you haven't turned eighteen yet?"

"I'd need Mom and Dad's consent."

That didn't sound like it was going to be easy.

"How are you going to convince them to let you marry Chuck when they think you're dating Tad? I mean, as far as Dad knows, Chuck is his old mechanic, not your boyfriend."

"Shit," she said. "I totally forgot about that."

She had asked me to keep their relationship a secret, and I had. Now it posed a problem.

"There's another option, but it may cause trouble," she said.

"What's the other option?" I asked.

Jeannie looked apprehensive. "Chuck's dad is a cop. He knows people. Chuck said if Mom and Dad say no, his dad can use his connections to bypass usual procedure."

Our parents would like that as much as a Soviet missile strike.

"I don't think that's a good idea," I warned. "Think of how upset Mom and Dad would be if you went behind their back."

Jeannie glanced at her belly. "If they say no, I won't have a choice."

I sighed. "Let's pray they don't say no then."

I couldn't believe all that had happened in less than twenty-four hours. It was madness. After putting the dishes in the sink to soak, I walked over to Jeannie and gave her a hug. "You still have to break it off with Tad."

Jeannie frowned. "That's going to be the hard part. He's so nice. He doesn't deserve to have his heart broken."

She seemed to genuinely care for Tad, and for a moment, I wondered if she would have married Tad and eventually found happiness if Chuck hadn't returned. I quickly dismissed the thought. Wasting time wondering about "what ifs" wasn't very productive. Still, I didn't envy her having to end things with Tad and then try to convince our parents to let her marry Chuck.

Jeannie checked the time. "I have to go to work. I'll talk to Tad afterward."

I had an idea on how I could help with our parents. Once I shared it with her, she agreed I should try it and let her know how it went. We hugged, she went her way, and I showered and went mine.

All I needed now was luck.

I knocked on my parent's door. Mom answered. "Hey, honey. Good to see you."

"You too," I said.

She had been watching her favorite daytime soap, so I joined her, not wanting to interrupt.

"This is almost over," she said.

I found it ironic we were watching a similar drama play out on screen.

When it finished, she turned to me. "Sorry about that. I just get so involved. It's like the people on the show are my friends."

I smiled. "I'm like that with books." I was feeling nervous all of a sudden, so I let out a deep breath as quietly as I could.

Mom's expression didn't change. "So, what's new?"

"So much. More like where to start."

That got her attention. "I just talked to you less than a week ago. What's going on?"

I leaned forward like I was telling her a secret. "I talked to Bernice the other day. Remember that boy she had a crush on in New Mexico, her neighbor's older brother?"

"Yeah."

"Well, they're dating now. I guess he finally noticed her now that she grew up."

"Aww. That's great news. I'm so happy for her."

She was smiling and in a good mood. Part one of the plan was a success.

"Yeah, she's thrilled." I paused and sat up straight. "But now Jeannie's got a dilemma."

Mom grew concerned. "A dilemma. What about?"

"I don't know if you know this because it's kind of been a secret, but Jeannie has always had eyes for Dad's mechanic, Chuck."

Mom looked surprised.

"But he was a little older, and then he left for Vietnam. She heard it through the grapevine he had gone missing, and no one knew his whereabouts. And as time passed, she eventually moved on and started dating Tad."

Mom hung on my every word.

"Turns out Chuck is alive, and he's come home."

Mom's jaw dropped. "I never knew anything about that," she whispered. She stared into space for a bit, thinking. She looked up. "That explains why Jeannie was so depressed for a while, remember?"

I pretended to make the connection. "Yeah. You're right. Now it all makes sense."

Mom sat up straighter and smoothed the front of her skirt. I gave her a few moments of triumph before I continued. "Anyway, Jeannie came over last night and asked me what she should do."

"And what did you tell her?"

"I told her she can't keep dating Tad, who, according to her, is serious and already talking marriage, if her heart is set on this other fellow. I told her she has to find a way to see Chuck, and soon, to figure things out. Who knows? She may not even like him anymore."

Mom nodded. "I agree. She may not feel the same once she sees him. And what if he doesn't have feelings for her? It's not always reciprocal, you know."

I realized my blunder and tried to correct it. "According to Jeannie, it is. She said they talked a few times and got along great. She kind of made it seem like they would eventually start dating, but then he got called to Vietnam."

Mom looked dumbfounded. "I can't believe we didn't know any of this," she said.

I thought of all she had missed and let out a nervous laugh. "I know. I never would have guessed." I cleared my throat. "But Jeannie's over the moon that he's returned. She's going to see him tonight."

My mind drifted to poor Tad. As if reading my thoughts, Mom said, "I kind of like Tad. I'd hate to see them break up."

"I know. I guess we'll just have to wait and see what happens."

Mom sighed. "To be young and in love," she said. "Well, all we can do is hope things turn out for the best."

We spent another hour snacking on coffee cake and talking about Dad's job and the apartment building. Then I left to head home and make dinner. Jeannie got off early and stopped by my place before heading to Tad's. I told her how it went with

Mom, and she thanked me. Prepping Mom and Dad would make what she had to say a little easier.

"Now, if only what I have to do next wasn't so hard," she said.

Chapter 24

I had just gotten out of the tub when I heard the phone ring. I ran for it because Jim had said he'd call before he came home to see if I needed anything from the store.

"Hello," I answered, out of breath.

"Lou. It's Mom," she said, sounding annoyed.

"Hey, Mom," I replied in an upbeat fashion. "How are you?"

"Not good," she answered.

"Why? What's the matter?"

"Are you sitting down?"

"Yes."

"Good. Because I have shocking news: your sister got married."

"How is that possible?" I asked, feigning ignorance.

"Because Chuck's dad is a police officer. Apparently, he pulled some strings so we didn't have to give consent. That's how," she snapped.

"He can do that?" I asked, feeling guilty about playing along.

"Yep. He's a cop, Lou. Apparently, laws don't apply to him."

I gulped. I had never heard her sound so angry. "I know you're upset, Mom, but there's nothing we can do. What's done is done. Remember last week when you said you hoped things turned out for the best?"

"I said I hoped things turned out for the best, as in she picked the right guy. I didn't want her to get married!" There was a pause. "And your father! He's furious. All he's done since he heard the news is curse Chuck's name and say someone should take his dad's badge."

This was a disaster of epic proportions. "Gosh, I don't know what to say, Mom. Do you guys want to come over so we can talk about it? I can make dinner—"

"No. But I appreciate it. Let's do it another time."

"Okay."

I took a moment to absorb everything we'd discussed. "So, where's Jeannie now?"

"Gone. After she told us she had gotten married, she packed her things and left. Said she's moving to Chuck's dad's house until they get a place of their own."

"I'm sorry you're angry, Mom. I'm sure Jeannie didn't do it to upset you or Dad. She's just young and in love."

"I know. But at the very least, I would have liked to have been invited to my own daughter's wedding. Is that too much to ask?" she said, her voice cracking.

Mom was right. Jeannie marrying Chuck behind their back was wrong. She should've at least told them first.

"No. It's not too much to ask. But my guess is Jeannie figured you'd say no, and it would cause a fight, and she was trying to avoid that."

I heard sniffling on the line.

"If she had asked, we would have said no." Mom paused. "She barely knows this man, and she's too young. Your father thinks her actions were impulsive."

I couldn't argue with that. And if it were under any other circumstances, I would have advised Jeannie to take it slow. "Well, let's just hope it was the right decision then, however rash."

When I hung up, I felt drained. The stunt Jeannie pulled in an attempt to avoid drama just ended up creating more. I rubbed my face, frustrated. As much as I loved Jeannie, she could be a pain in the butt sometimes.

I told Jim the story over dinner.

"It's so crazy that she ran off and got married without telling anyone," he said.

It was crazy, but I didn't want to discuss it with him. "When it comes to love, people are unpredictable. Jeannie's no different, I guess."

Jim smiled at me. "You're a good sister, Lou. Forgiving and kind."

"I'm that way with my sister, but if one of our kids pulls that crap on us, I'll be pissed."

That got Jim laughing so hard he almost choked on his food. Once he'd calmed down, he said, "You want help with the dishes?"

I raised an eyebrow.

"So you have energy for babymaking," he clarified in the velvety voice that had won me over the day we met.

The following day I was having coffee when the doorbell rang. I checked the peephole and saw Jeannie.

"I heard you got hitched," I said.

"And how'd that conversation go?" she asked, eyeing me anxiously.

"You should have asked them first. Mom was so upset she was crying."

Jeannie crossed her arms. "I didn't ask because I knew they'd say no. I figured there was no point."

"You were right about that. They would have said no. But by not asking them and just going and doing it, Dad is furious, and Mom is going on about how she wasn't invited to her own daughter's wedding."

Jeannie's glow was replaced with a scowl. "But if they wouldn't have given their consent, they wouldn't have come to the ceremony."

I sat on the sofa. "They're heartbroken. That's all. Think of it from their point of view. Their little girl ran off and married a guy they've never been formally introduced to. No one asked their permission, and then you showed up, packed your things, and left."

She plopped down on the couch. "There was just no winning," she murmured.

"Don't worry. They'll come around. Just give them a chance

to cool off. Think how happy they'll be when they hear about the baby."

Jeannie nodded. "I guess you're right." She was quiet for a minute before saying, "Everything just happened so fast. Chuck's dad got in touch with a buddy of his out in Oak Park who said he could marry us, but it had to be that day because he was booked solid the rest of the week. So I rushed to get ready and just managed to look presentable by the time we had to leave. On the way over, I regretted not calling you. I really wanted you to be there, but I guess it wasn't meant to be."

"Considering how upset Mom and Dad were, maybe it was good I didn't go. They might have gotten upset with me too."

"True." Jeannie appeared lost in a private thought and smiled, her earlier happiness returning. "I'm just glad I was able to marry him. He's so..." She giggled. "You know."

I did know. Jim was like that for me.

As I sat with Jeannie, I thought about the baby on its way and how I planned to have one too. Jim and I just hadn't had any luck yet. But as he said, there was no rush. We were young and had plenty of time.

A month later, Jeannie still hadn't been able to mend things with our parents. Chuck's dad had invited them over for dinner, but they'd declined, still perturbed over his prior actions. And Dad had gotten into the habit of calling Chuck a sneaky bastard.

I followed Jim's advice and stayed out of it. Plus, I was busy. Jim and his dad needed new appliances for the second apartment building they were buying. While out shopping for the best bargain, I let the issue slip my mind.

I was becoming a respected visitor at some of the stores. They no longer waited on me like a regular customer. I had my own salesman who set appointments and was able to get me bulk discounts approved by the store manager.

Jim snuggled up to me on the couch. "They give you discounts because you're cute."

"And here I thought it was because I was a hotshot businesswoman."

"You are hot," he teased, biting my earlobe.

I pulled away.

"What's wrong?" he asked.

I pouted. "I want to be a businesswoman."

Jim burst out laughing.

"What's so funny?" I asked, feeling offended.

"You are. You're so focused on wanting to be a businesswoman you don't even realize you already are one."

I gazed at him. "You really think so?"

He smiled and gave me a kiss on the lips. "I know so." He sat back. "And I know just the thing to prove it. I'm going to have business cards made for you. That will make it official."

"Business cards, for me?" I asked.

"Yes. Business cards for you. The smartest woman I know."

I swelled with pride. If only Bernice could see me now.

Chapter 25

When Jeannie announced she was pregnant, everything changed. After some raised eyebrows and unspoken questions about the timing of the baby, my parents warmed to the idea of becoming grandparents, and the ugly business of how Chuck and Jeannie had snuck off to get married became a thing of the past.

Mom invited Chuck to dinner for the first time and asked Jim and me to come along. She said she wanted it to be a whole family celebration, but I also imagine she wanted everyone there so it would be less uncomfortable. That was fine by me because I was more than happy for life to return to normal.

We all sat around the table.

"How's the car?" Chuck asked Dad.

"Runs like a charm," he answered.

There was a long awkward silence. Dad broke it not with accusations or judgment about Chuck and Jeannie but with a moment of levity.

"But if I have any troubles, I know where to go." He smiled politely at Chuck, and Chuck nodded.

"How are things going at the factory?" Jim asked Jeannie. "You think you'll stay on until the end, or…"

Jeannie finished chewing her food and blotted her face with a napkin. "I think I'll stay for a few more months, until I'm too big to sit and sew for that many hours."

"Yeah. I would think that would be uncomfortable," Jim added.

Instead of silently stuffing his face as most men did, Jim went out of his way to create conversation, making the night a lot less awkward. On the way over, we had decided it was best not to talk about Vietnam, and thankfully, Mom and Dad managed to avoid the topic as well.

After more tension-relieving light banter, Chuck went outside with Jim to admire his car, and Dad sat on the sofa, keeping Jeannie company. Mom and I retreated to the kitchen to do dishes.

"Do you think it's a girl or a boy?" Mom asked as she handed me a plate to dry.

"I don't know. But I think she'd prefer a girl. She thinks they're easier to raise."

Mom gave me a look that refuted the statement and continued scrubbing the glass she had in her hand. After a few minutes of silence, she said, "Seems like Jeannie got pregnant right away, huh?"

"Yeah, some people have all the luck," I said.

She turned to me. "Don't worry. It will happen to you, too."

I managed a small smile. It was easy to say "don't worry" when you had kids and weren't the one trying to get pregnant. Still, I knew her intentions were good.

"How's Jim's dad been?" Mom asked, changing the subject.

"The same. Likes to stay busy and keeps to himself." Mom and Dad thought it was odd he didn't date anyone. A few years had passed since his divorce, and most men wouldn't just be dating, they'd be remarried by then. Jim's dad spent all his time working.

"Well…your father knows someone who's just been through a divorce, too. She's a nice lady."

"I'll mention it to Jim on the way home."

So I did. Jim's response was to giggle.

"What's so funny?" I asked.

"I'm picturing my dad's face when I tell him your parents are playing matchmaker. He'll look like he's just eaten broken glass, then he'll say what he always says, that women are the devil."

I pictured his dad's face all screwed up and laughed, too. "Seriously, though. He can't feel that way about everyone."

Jim turned onto our street. "I assure you, he does. Mom really broke his heart. And I don't think he's going to take a chance on anyone else. Least of all someone we suggest." He parked the car and pulled the keys from the ignition. "If he meets someone, it has to happen on its own."

After giving it some thought, I decided I wouldn't like to go on a blind date, even if I hadn't gone through a nasty divorce. Jim was right. If it happened, it would have to happen on its own.

Later on, as I watched Jim go through the mail, I wondered if he'd ever talk to his mom again. The few times I'd brought it up, he said he didn't want to discuss her, so I stopped mentioning it.

I spoke to Bernice right before the holidays. She had been hoping to come home for Christmas, but it was just too expensive. "I'll see you on summer break. Jeannie will have had the baby by then, right?"

"Right." Bernice and I hadn't been in touch as often as we used to, but with Bernice, it didn't matter how much time had passed. We always picked up right where we had left off.

"Mom thinks it's going to be a boy since she's carrying low. What do you think?" I asked.

"I think that's an old wives' tale," she scoffed.

"Probably. But enough about Jeannie. How's school? How's Alejandro?"

"School is hard. There's so much homework. And I only see Alejandro on the weekends."

"So every week, you can't wait until Friday, am I right?" I asked, giggling.

"It's all I think about when I'm not studying. And sometimes when I am," she said. "I'm ready to go all the way and get it over with already so that I can think straight."

"Maybe it would help your grade point average," I joked.

Bernice cracked up. "It probably would."

After we hung up, I realized I had forgotten to tell her about my new business cards. I reached for my purse, pulled one out of the ornate silver case I had them stored in, and smiled. I'd have to send one with her Christmas card.

***

The first few months of 1963 were filled with running Jeannie to doctor appointments, shopping for the baby with my mom, and helping Jeannie and Chuck find a place to live. Jim had suggested a unit at the second building since it was close to Chuck's work, and after looking the place over, they accepted.

"We can afford to give them a decent discount," Jim said, and when he saw how happy the news made me, he leaned in and kissed me on the forehead. "I think you should use your clout at the furniture store for the interior, too."

"I'll have to see what they want to spend first." Jeannie had stopped working at the factory, but they had managed to save money while living at Chuck's dad's house, so I wasn't worried.

"I'm sure they're in good hands," he added, patting me on the behind as I got up to leave.

Mom, Jeannie, and I had finished shopping and were relaxing at my place when Jeannie's water broke.

"I'll call Chuck," Mom said, rushing to the phone.

Chaos ensued, with Mom and I rushing to and fro, and Jeannie looking horrified.

"I'm so sorry. I can't believe this happened on the sofa," Jeannie said.

"It's just fabric. It'll clean," I assured her, reaching for her arm to help her up. I heard Chuck's car, and a moment later, he burst through the door, looking frantic.

Jeannie and Chuck sped off, and I gave Jim a call. He said he'd pick us up as soon as he was finished with his appointment.

Mom paced back and forth, biting her nails. I did the same thing in the opposite direction, realizing I must have picked up the habit from her. Jim showed up not long afterward, and we drove to the hospital.

When we arrived, a nurse directed us, and I saw Chuck in the waiting area.

"How is she?" I asked him.

Just then, I heard Jeannie shriek in pain from behind closed doors.

"It's been like that for the last twenty minutes," he said. His face was sheet white.

"Are you doing okay?" I asked.

Chuck exhaled loudly. "I've been through unspeakable things, but it's different when it's someone you love hurting."

"I understand." I wished I could say something to comfort him.

Mom poked her head in the room to get a glimpse of Jeannie, and as she did, Jeannie let out a blood-curdling scream that echoed down the hall.

Chuck stiffened. He looked like he was about to snap.

"Have you eaten anything?" Jim asked.

"No," he replied, his voice tight.

"You want to go across the street and grab some food? If Jeannie has the baby while we're gone, Lou will come and get us. If not, we'll still have enjoyed a hot meal."

Chuck appeared to consider his offer. And as he weighed the pros and cons, trying to make a decision, the doctor came out.

Everyone turned to him, breathless.

The doctor reached for Chuck's hand and shook it.

"Congratulations," the doctor said. "You are the proud father of a baby girl."

Chapter 26

Being a new mother proved a challenge for Jeannie. She was overwhelmed and exhausted, so I stopped by often to do what I could to help her out. One day, after I'd finished making a casserole for their dinner, I stood behind Jeannie and began brushing her hair.

"She's beautiful, isn't she?" Jeannie said, glancing at Lisa sleeping in her crib.

"She sure is." Jeannie stared into the distance. Worry lines creased her forehead.

"You okay?" I asked.

"Yeah. I'm just feeling a little guilty." She turned to face me. "Our baby is so precious, you know, but I can't help but think that she's not really ours."

Jeannie had crossed paths with Tad a few times since the breakup. The first time, he had been a gentleman and wished her happiness in her new life with Chuck. On the second run-in, when it was apparent she was pregnant, he had congratulated her and told her she'd make a wonderful mother. Each time she saw him, she felt worse. And now that Lisa was born, it seemed to bother her even more.

"She is yours," I said. "You decided to follow your heart. And you have to learn to live with that decision."

Jeannie locked eyes with me, seeming to realize for the first time it would weigh on her conscience for the rest of her life, and wordlessly nodded acceptance.

Lisa stirred in her crib, grabbing our attention. Jeannie went over and picked her up, smiling and making cooing sounds, her prior worries forgotten.

For the moment.

***

Summer approached, and I couldn't wait for Bernice to come home. I gave her a call, anxious to catch up.

"The baby's doing great," I reported. "Jeannie's getting the swing of things and doesn't need help anymore."

"That's good to hear."

She didn't sound as excited as I thought she'd be. She was quiet for a bit, then said, "I've got some good news, and I've got some bad news."

"What's the bad news?" I asked.

"I'm not coming back to Chicago this summer."

"What? How come?"

"Because I'm getting married!" she squealed. "What do you say, Lou? Will you be my maid of honor?"

I was at a loss for words. "Of course!" I answered once the shock wore off. "Of course, I will. This is such great news!"

"You won't believe how he asked me. It was so romantic."

"Tell me," I demanded.

There was a clattering sound, and Bernice returned, laughing. "Sorry. The phone slipped out of my hand." Bernice exhaled. "We were hiking in the mountains, and he said he wanted to show me something, a special spot, he'd said. So we continued up to a ridge with a scenic overlook. It was so beautiful, it took my breath away. I was just about to tell him how pretty it was when he reached for my hand, got down on one knee, and asked me to marry him."

"Wow! I'll bet that really took your breath away. It's so romantic. Like a chapter in your uncle's book."

"I know," she replied, giddy with excitement.

I marked the wedding date in my calendar, and we discussed bridesmaid dresses and shoes, both of which she said she'd order locally after getting my measurements.

"Juan is going to be the best man. So you'll be standing up together," she said.

I was happy I'd finally get to meet her neighbor and soon-to-be brother-in-law. "Let me talk to Jim and we'll either get airline tickets or drive. I can't wait!"

We chatted a little while longer, then hung up. Afterward, I sat on the sofa and felt a wave of sadness wash over me. Bernice had gone to school out west, and now she was getting married to a man that had said he would never leave New Mexico.

That could mean only one thing: I had just lost my best friend.

I went to the bathroom and filled the tub. As I soaked in the hot water, tears flowed. I thought of all the fun times Bernice and I had growing up and found it hard to believe we wouldn't be able to see each other from now on. I pictured her living out west, married to a man who lived on a ranch with horses, and smiled. I couldn't think of anyone I'd rather have living my childhood dream than Bernice.

When Jim got home, I told him the good news.

He hugged me. "Are you all right?" he asked.

"I will be," I said, not wanting to let him go.

Jim rubbed my back. "Let's go out to dinner tonight. Why don't you put on a nice dress, and we'll try out someplace new. I'll put the food you made in the fridge, and we'll eat it tomorrow."

"Okay," I said, kissing him on the cheek. I went to my closet. There was a fancy frock I'd regretted buying because I didn't think I'd wear it often enough. I put it on and touched up my hair and make-up.

Halfway through our meal and bottle of wine, Jim gazed at me, glassy-eyed. "We should drive to New Mexico. Make a sightseeing trip of it. What do you think?"

"Sounds good to me," I grinned.

I had never told him about my dream to live out west because I didn't want him to think the life he'd given me was lacking in any way. The truth was he had provided everything I had ever wanted, and I couldn't be happier.

"I'll have to buy a new suit," he said. "And have Chuck tune up the car before we leave."

Jim was more than capable of working on his own car but faithfully took it to Chuck ever since he became family. As we shared dessert, I felt thankful that my husband was as thoughtful as he was smart.

And even though I'd miss Bernice, I was glad we both had gotten lucky in love.

***

A week before the wedding, Jim's dad came down with pneumonia. He had a high fever, and Jim was concerned about leaving him.

"I can't believe this is happening right now," Jim said, clearly torn. "I hate to say this, but I don't think I should go with you."

I felt terrible leaving when his dad was so ill, but I couldn't miss Bernice's wedding.

Jim rubbed his chin, thinking. "Here's what we're going to do," he finally said. "I'm going to stay behind with my dad, and you're going to fly to New Mexico."

I'd never been on a plane before, and the idea of flying alone terrified me.

"Don't worry," he said after seeing my reaction. "Flying is safe. And I'll make sure to mention it's your first time in the air so you get special attention."

"Okay." I nodded, still scared.

Jim grabbed the phone book and found the number to call and book the flight. Once he had finished, I called Bernice and let her know of the change of plans.

"I'm sorry to hear about your father-in-law," she said. "Horrible timing."

"I know."

"Let me check my schedule," she said. I heard her flipping

the pages of her calendar. "Looks like I've got a final dress fitting the time your flight arrives. Would you mind if I sent Juan to pick you up?"

Great. First, I had to soar through the sky cross country without my husband, and then a stranger would pick me up at the airport and take me to Bernice's, all while I worried about my ailing father-in-law.

"No. I don't mind," I said unconvincingly. "But how will he know who I am?"

"Good question." Bernice thought about it for a bit. "I know. I'll show him your picture. And just so you know it's him, I'll have him holding a sign with your name on it."

I didn't like the plan but didn't want to be difficult. "Are you sure he won't mind?"

"I'm positive. In fact, he'll probably think it's fun."

"If you say so," I said. How someone could think waiting for someone they didn't know while holding a sign could be fun, I didn't know, but I kept that thought to myself.

"And how about my dress? It's ready, right?" I asked.

"Ready and waiting."

"And you got the check I sent?"

"I got the check, and everything's all set," Bernice said.

"Okay, then. See you soon."

I laughed to myself. I was frazzled, and I wasn't the one getting married. Bernice, on the other hand, was unruffled; her wedding was just another piece in the puzzle of her life falling into place.

Chapter 27

Jim's dad was still bedridden when it was time for me to leave for New Mexico. I had suggested taking a cab to the airport, but Jim wanted to take me himself. On the way there, I kept thinking of how close Jim and his dad were and prayed he would get better soon.

Once Jim helped me get checked in, he gave me a big hug and a kiss. "Have fun," he said. "And tell Bernice how sorry I am that I couldn't make it."

I looked up at him, still more than a little frightened. "I will," I murmured.

He smiled and waved goodbye as I boarded, and before I knew it, I was sitting in my seat, trying to act calm as I watched the stewardess' safety presentation like I would be quizzed on it afterward.

My stomach felt a little queasy as the plane went through minor turbulence. I closed my eyes in an attempt to block everything out and wished I could have driven to New Mexico with Bernice's parents, but they had left before Jim's dad got sick.

After landing, I kept my eyes peeled for Juan. Bernice had described him as a walking smile and said to look for a set of white teeth, and I'd spot him right away.

I trailed an old man who moved at a snail-like pace, then scanned the waiting group of people. Finally, I saw a dark-skinned man holding a sign. I couldn't read what was written on it from where I was standing, but I saw the big smile and headed in his direction.

I saw the name Lou written in black ink on white cardboard as I got closer. "You must be Juan," I said, stopping in front of him.

"The one and only." He tossed the sign into a nearby

garbage can and shook my hand. "So nice to finally meet you." His smile got even brighter.

"Likewise," I said, following him to baggage claim.

He grabbed my suitcase and turned to me. "Have you eaten?"

I had skipped breakfast because I was nervous about the flight, and now that it was late afternoon, I was starving. My stomach growled loudly in confirmation, and Juan laughed.

"That answers that," he said.

I felt my cheeks flush, but before I could say anything, he added, "I know just the place. Bernice and I go there all the time."

We stepped outside, and I got my first look at the west. The sky was clear and blue in a way I'd never seen before, and the air was warm and dry. Mountains loomed on my right-hand side, and I gazed at them and sighed.

Juan saw me glancing around. "Not much to see," he said. "We're just a small town compared to Chicago."

"I think it's beautiful," I said, climbing into his truck after he tossed my luggage in the back. Juan started the engine, which sputtered at first, then came to life.

"Bernice told me you'd say that," he said.

Once we got to the restaurant, Juan ordered for us. "Bring us both cheese enchiladas. Christmas. But put hers on the side." It sounded like he was speaking a foreign language, and I was glad he had suggested ordering for me.

The waitress brought us two glasses of water and a basket of chips and salsa. Ravenous, I bit into a chip, which was greasy and warm, and took a sip of my drink.

"This salsa is mild," Juan assured me, so I dipped my second chip into it and took a bite. It was delicious but not mild according to my taste buds.

Our food arrived shortly after that, and I tasted both the green and red chile, which were on the side as instructed. Both tasted hot.

"Do you remember you were supposed to come here that one summer?" Juan asked.

"Yeah," I said, taking a gulp of water in an attempt to extinguish the fire in my mouth. "I'm still pissed my parents wouldn't let me come."

Juan laughed. "Don't feel bad. I wanted to go on vacation to Chicago and never made it there, either. So we've got something in common."

I thought it was funny we felt the same way about our home states but didn't mention it.

"But we're going to have fun now," he promised, slapping his hand on the table. "The ladies have been busy cooking up a storm for the wedding. It's a guaranteed blast."

His enthusiasm was infectious. I couldn't wait to see Bernice.

Juan had the windows rolled down as we drove up to Santa Fe, causing the mini wind chimes that hung from his rearview mirror to clink together lightly. The peaceful sound combined with jet lag and a full belly lulled me to sleep. I didn't wake up until I heard Bernice whisper, "Wake up, sleepyhead," in my ear.

My eyes popped open. "Ahhhh!" I squealed. I jumped out of the truck and gave her a bone-crushing hug. "I can't believe I fell asleep!"

Bernice released me, and we smiled at each other. It felt just like old times but out west.

"She snores," Juan exclaimed, causing us to break into a fit of laughter.

Bernice swatted his arm, and he grinned as a taller Hispanic man came out from inside the house.

"Louise. I'm Alejandro. So nice to meet you." He extended his hand, and I shook it, amazed at how good-looking he was. We exchanged pleasantries, and Juan and Alejandro went inside, taking my luggage with them.

"What do you think?" Bernice asked, wanting my opinion of her future husband.

"I think you hit the jackpot."

"I know," she said, gripping my arm. "I can't wait until the wedding night."

I loved seeing Bernice act like a love-crazed female instead of a bookworm. "Only two more nights," I reminded her, winking.

A woman with long, wavy gray hair wearing a colorful dress and cowboy boots opened the front door.

"This is my aunt," Bernice said.

"The name's Grace," the woman added.

I smiled and said, "Nice to meet you."

Bernice showed me the room I'd be staying in, and afterward, I asked her if it would be okay if I called Jim.

"Of course," she said, showing me to the phone.

He answered on the second ring. "I'm so glad you're okay. I was kind of worried," he confessed.

"I'm fine," I assured him. "How's your dad doing?"

"His fever finally came down."

"Thank God."

"I know. It's nice to see him looking a little better. So how's your day been?"

I told him about the flight and finding Juan holding the sign. I described the delicious, spicy meal we'd eaten before heading to Santa Fe, and finally, smiling, I confessed that Juan had told everyone I'd fallen asleep and snored on the ride up.

Jim was silent for a moment. "Sounds like you're having a good time," he said.

"I am." I yawned. "Just a little tired. Juan said it takes a while to get used to the elevation."

"Hmm. Well, get some rest," he suggested. "You've had a long day."

"Bernice and I are staying in tonight, just the two of us, but I'll probably go to bed early."

"Okay. Goodnight then," he said, giving me a phone kiss. I kissed him back and hung up.

Aunt Grace eyed me. "Checked in with the man in charge, did you?" Her voice sounded gravelly, like she'd smoked too many cigarettes.

I let out a nervous laugh. "It's not like that."

"It's always like that," she smirked, "Trust me." She gave me a knowing smile I didn't dare question, then Bernice came to my rescue.

"Don't let her scare you," she said. "She's just jaded."

"Your uncle had that effect on me." Grace cursed as she walked away. Her gait was uneven, like a drunkard, but I hadn't smelled alcohol on her breath.

I glanced at Bernice, confused. I thought she said her uncle had died a long time ago.

"She's fine," she said, dismissing her.

We went to Bernice's room to have some privacy. After she shut the door, she said, "My aunt's best friend is a feminist. They're both obsessed with Betty Friedan's *The Feminine Mystique*. Sometimes they smoke together."

I was still confused, but suddenly, it hit me. "Oh!" I said.

Bernice shook her head and smiled. "She's harmless."

I hadn't met anyone like Bernice's aunt before. She seemed a little strange, but if Bernice said she was fine, I'd take her word for it. I noted Bernice's parents had chosen to stay at a hotel instead of at the house and wondered if they thought she was harmless too, or if they just wanted to spend some quality time alone.

Bernice and I changed into pajamas and spent the rest of the night talking. I had missed her, and even though I was tired, I found enough energy to stay up well past when we should have gone to bed, talking about everything under the sun. I said a prayer before I fell asleep, asking that we continue to see each other through the years and stay close.

Chapter 28

The next day Bernice, her aunt, and I took care of some last-minute wedding details, one of which was to make sure my dress and shoes fit. As we drove through town, I was struck by how different Santa Fe was compared to Chicago. The city was tiny, with buildings that looked to be made of mud and streets that went every which way. The women dressed flamboyantly, and the men wore cowboy boots and hats. It was like being in a foreign country.

We met Bernice's parents for lunch, and after saying hello, I scanned the menu and realized it was more Mexican food. I ordered my chile on the side, remembering Juan's suggestion, and when my food came, I was disappointed to find it was still too hot to eat. I picked at my meal, all while watching Bernice's parents interact with her aunt, who seemed less opinionated today and easier to be around.

I was drowsy on the ride back to the ranch. I thought I had gotten used to the elevation but still felt a little lightheaded. When Grace parked the car, I opened my eyes and saw Juan and Alejandro standing outside.

"Wake up, sleepyhead," Juan teased as I stepped out.

I yawned. "I don't know what's wrong with me. I'm never like this."

Alejandro smiled. "Don't worry, Lou. We've got just the thing to cure you."

I raised an eyebrow and glanced at Bernice.

"We're going horseback riding," she said. "The guys do it all the time, and my parents were interested, and you—"

"I've always wanted to!" I exclaimed with the exuberance of a small child.

"You've never ridden?" Juan asked.

"No."

"Hmm. Well, I'm going to give you a choice then. I can put you on a horse that's mild-mannered and great for beginners, or you can ride with me on *Trueno.*"

A few of the Spanish vocabulary words stuck with me. "Thunder?" I asked.

"Yes. That's correct," Juan said, impressed.

With a name like Thunder, I knew the horse would be fast, and that if I took him up on his offer, I'd get to gallop at a pace I'd never be able to experience on my own. I hemmed and hawed, unsure if it was a good idea for a married woman to ride with a relative stranger.

"You're not chicken, are you?" Juan asked. Alejandro stood next to him and snickered.

Bernice elbowed him to stop. "C'mon, guys. Let Lou choose whichever horse she wants. Not everyone is looking for an adrenalin rush."

"I'll try Thunder," I blurted. That was exactly what I wanted – an adrenalin rush.

"Good choice," Juan said. "We'll meet you by the barn when you're ready."

Bernice and I headed to the house to change clothes.

"You don't have to ride Thunder if you don't want to," she said. "Juan is just joking. Don't feel like—"

"I want to ride Thunder. Really. It sounds like fun."

"Okay." She smiled. "Let me give you something comfortable to wear."

I changed into pants and a shirt and slipped on appropriate shoes before meeting Bernice and her parents on the porch. Grace said she went horseback riding all the time and decided to pass, preferring to stay home and do housework.

Bernice gave Alejandro a kiss and mounted her horse. Afterward, Alejandro showed Bernice's mom how to correctly mount the horse she'd chosen and explained some of the basics as Bernice's dad listened, prepared to do the same with his.

Juan approached me and smiled. "You ready?" he asked.

"Absolutely," I said, standing tall and feeling confident.

"Okay. There's only one thing you have to remember." He locked eyes with me to make sure I was paying attention. "Hold on tight and don't let go."

"Understood."

The horses Bernice's parents were on had already started strolling alongside Bernice and Alejandro's horses. They had been interested in a relaxing ride, just to say they had done it once, and by the happy expressions on their faces, it looked like they were getting just what they wanted.

Juan took me to meet Thunder. "This is my friend, Lou. We're going to show her a good time. Okay?"

The chocolate brown horse and I made eye contact. His eyes flickered with fire, mirroring how I felt inside. Juan mounted and pulled me up behind him. I wrapped my arms around his waist as instructed and stole a final glance at Bernice. She grinned at me, and then I heard Juan say "Yah," and the horse darted forward, causing me to hold him tighter.

The wind whipped through my hair as we galloped through the fast-moving brown and green landscape. I closed my eyes and listened to the sound of Thunder's hooves hitting the ground and was mesmerized by the echoing pattern. Then, as the sun warmed my face, I took a deep breath of fresh mountain air and never felt more alive.

"You awake now?" Juan hollered as we propelled onward.

"Yes!" I shouted, a smile plastered to my face.

We had left the rest of our group in the dust and were racing down the side of a hill toward a narrow stream. As we got closer, Juan commanded Thunder to slow. At the water's edge, Thunder stopped, and Juan and I climbed down and stretched while Thunder took a drink.

Juan looked at me and nodded approval. "You've got spunk, Lou. I like that."

"When I was a kid, it was called being headstrong. It usually ended in a spanking or being sent to my room."

Juan laughed. "The good old days, huh?"

I laughed, too. They were indeed good. Thunder neighed, grabbing our attention.

I went over and reached out to touch his silky mane. "You're so sweet, aren't you," I said in the voice I used when talking to small children. Thunder glanced at me and slightly shook his head as if showing off.

"What a ham," Juan said. "And look at him. He's standing completely still so you can pet him. He never does that."

"He likes me," I said.

Juan nodded and let out a deep sigh. "I guess we should be heading back," he said.

As Juan helped me onto the horse, I prepared myself for another heart-pounding experience. But instead of speeding home, Juan had Thunder canter at a moderate pace, which was perfect for sightseeing. There were mountains as far as the eye could see, with the occasional home dotting the vast landscape. A lone cloud hung in the electric blue sky. Rays streaked through its center, expanding like fingers in all directions.

I could get used to this, I thought. And as quickly as I had the idea, I let it slip away.

When Juan and I returned to the barn, the rest of the party was there waiting, wearing big smiles.

"Holy cow, Lou! You should have seen you two. It was just like in the movies," Bernice said.

I grinned from ear to ear. "I know, right? It was a once in a lifetime experience." I turned to Juan. "Thanks so much for taking me."

"My pleasure," he said.

After dinner, Bernice's parents went back to the hotel, and we had some time alone. I asked her to follow me to the guest bedroom and pulled a wrapped box from my luggage.

"Sorry...the corner got a little smashed." I handed it to her.

Bernice took it from me and ripped the paper off. She lifted the dark purple silk nighty inside.

"Not wedding night apparel but something sexy in your favorite color."

"I love it," she said. "I'm going to wear it tomorrow."

"You mean you don't have something planned to wear already?" I asked, surprised.

"I do. But this is better. He won't be expecting this," she said, wearing a wicked grin.

The girl had gone from hustling pennies to hitting the books. Next, she would master the art of seduction. I had no doubt she'd become an expert.

Bernice suggested we sit outside, so I followed her to the front porch. It was a wraparound kind with a bench and two rocking chairs. We sat next to each other in silence, rocking slowly as we gazed at the night sky, which was pitch black and filled with stars.

"I'm going to miss you when I leave," I said, a melancholy feeling coming over me.

"I'm going to miss you, too." She sighed. "It's funny, isn't it? How things turn out."

"What do you mean?" I asked.

Bernice turned to me. "You know. Me being out here when it was your dream of moving out west and marrying a man with horses and a ranch." She shook her head. "The irony is Juan thinks you're the greatest thing on two legs, but you're already taken."

Chapter 29

The morning of the wedding, I woke up both excited and conflicted. I was standing up with Juan, and although we'd been having a lot of fun, I didn't want to give him the wrong idea. I put on my eyeliner, and as I started applying mascara, decided not to fret. I was leaving tomorrow anyway, and it wasn't like he was pursuing me; it was just a comment Bernice had made in passing.

I drove with Grace and Bernice to the church, a large one in town called St. Francis Cathedral. It was the tallest building in the area, a Romanesque Revival Grace had said, and it stood out amongst the adobe buildings.

Bernice's parents were waiting out front. We said hello to them and went inside. Her parents joined Alejandro's, and she and I took our places until the ceremony started. My dress felt tight as I stood and admired the inside of the church. Alejandro's three cousins, who were also standing up in the wedding, fidgeted with their dresses as well.

A pianist began playing, cueing it was time to start. Next, the younger cousins paired up with their male counterparts and took practiced, measured steps down the aisle. Then it was my turn. Juan had a serious look on his face as he stood by my side, and then he nodded, and we began walking down the aisle.

I stood next to the female wedding attendants and held my breath as I watched Bernice approach, arm in arm with her father. Emotions welled up, and tears filled my eyes even though I had sworn I wouldn't cry. I took a few deep breaths and was able to hold them back, but as the priest said, "I now proclaim you man and wife," a few escaped.

We went back to the ranch after taking pictures. The yard had been transformed with a large white canopy covering tables decorated with white roses and candles. Alejandro's parents, aunts, and uncles had been working hard behind the scenes to make every detail just right, and from what I could see, they had done a stellar job.

The food was set out buffet-style on a long table so we could pick what we wanted, and hungry guests lined up behind Bernice and Alejandro, filling their plates with a little bit of everything.

"Try that dish," Juan said, pointing. "Mom made that one mild." I didn't see him come up behind me and was slightly startled.

"I think your definition of 'mild' and mine are two very different things," I said in a low voice so only he could hear.

Juan laughed. "If you say so." He scooped a portion from the other tray onto his plate. "Now, this is the good stuff," he said.

I scanned the other dishes and took a small portion of each. "That's all you're eating?" he asked.

"I'm using dinner as an appetizer for dessert, which I'm planning to make the main course."

"I hate to break it to you, but there's chile in the cake, too," Juan deadpanned.

"No!" I frowned. "I've been looking forward to eating something sweet."

"I'm kidding." He grinned. "What? You think we put chile in everything?"

I pursed my lips. "I wouldn't put it past you."

Juan and I went to sit at the main table with Alejandro and Bernice, and when everyone was seated, Alejandro's dad stood and made a toast. We clinked glasses and took a sip of champagne, and as we were about to eat, Juan stood. "I'd like to say a little something, too. I'll keep it brief so our food doesn't get cold." A few in the crowd giggled, then he said, "I just want to say I'm thrilled my brother married Bernice. She's an amazing woman and a great friend. I wish you both a lifetime of happiness." Guests raised their glasses again, and everyone dug in.

"So, when did you get married?" Juan asked me.

My neck muscles tensed. "A year ago," I answered.

Juan nodded and appeared to give my answer some thought while eyeing the guests.

"This is nice," he said. "I'd be happy with a wedding like this."

"Yeah. It's been wonderful. The church was mind-blowing. The ranch is beautiful. You can't ask for anything more."

Juan sighed. "Now, all I need is that special someone."

I made eye contact and smiled. "I'm sure you'll find her."

One of Juan's aunts stood and said it was time to cut the cake. Bernice and Alejandro rose and went toward her, holding hands. After they had done their ritual, his aunt expertly sliced and passed out pieces for each guest.

Juan and I returned to the table with ours.

"Now you can finally eat," he said.

I grinned and stabbed my fork into my piece, and took a bite. The cake was moist and sweet and decadent, and most importantly, it didn't scorch my tongue. Juan seemed to be enjoying his just as much, and I was thankful he didn't notice I had finished my slice before he had finished his.

"How do you like the dessert?" I heard Bernice ask from down the table.

I leaned forward so we could see each other. "I could eat the whole cake," I said. She giggled and shook her head.

"I didn't know you had such a sweet tooth," she said.

"Must be the company," I answered, then immediately corrected my faux pas, "I mean the occasion."

I heard Juan stifle a laugh next to me.

Bernice's new in-laws had hired a band for the reception. During dinner, they had played slow songs as a kind of gentle background music. Then, when everyone had finished eating dessert, they took a short intermission, announcing they'd play the first song for the bride and groom when they returned.

Fifteen minutes later, they came back and began softly strumming their Spanish guitars. I had never heard the tune and was trying to figure out what it was but gave up on it, preferring to watch Bernice and Alejandro stare with intensity into each other's eyes as they swayed from side to side.

The song ended, and Juan turned to me. "Since we're standing up together, we're supposed to dance together," he said.

"Yes, of course."

The next song was a slow one too, and instead of pulling me close, Juan took my hand in his and placed his other one high on my waist like a gentleman. His cousins paired up, surrounding us, and for a moment, I felt like family.

"You know we're drinking tonight, right?" Juan stated matter of factly.

"When you say we, do you mean you and me?"

"Yes. It's your last night here and your best friend's wedding. You can sleep the hangover off on the flight home."

I considered protesting but changed my mind. He was right. This was the time to live it up.

The song ended, and Juan led me to Alejandro and Bernice. Apparently, they had agreed to do one shot of the good tequila his dad had saved from a trip to Mexico, but no more as they didn't want to get drunk on their wedding night. After Juan said something to the bartender in Spanish, he reached down, pulled out a bottle, and poured each of us a shot.

Alejandro lifted his shot glass. "To Bernice. The woman of my dreams. My wife."

Bernice beamed at him for a beat, and we downed our drinks in unison. A rush of heat warmed my insides.

"Good. No?" Juan asked me.

"Very good." I remembered the two glasses of champagne I had earlier and hoped the liquors would mix well, dismissing the thought when the band began playing a fast song.

"Let's dance," Bernice said to me.

We stepped onto the dance floor, a wooden platform painted white, and I quickly felt intimidated by the dance moves of her new relatives. They all swiveled their hips and glided around with grace, where Bernice and I moved with more awkward, angular motions. Bernice's parents danced nearby, looking happy and unconcerned with their skills, and when they saw me glancing their way, waved and smiled.

When the song ended, Bernice went to chat with her parents and aunt, and I got another piece of cake. Juan came and sat down next to me, looking bored.

"It'll all be over soon," he said, sounding a little sad.

The thought of leaving made me sad, too. Bernice and I had promised to visit each other as often as possible, but who knew how much we'd really get to see each other? Jim had reminded me we always had the phone, which I was grateful for, but it just wasn't the same.

I turned to Juan. "I thought we were going to drink. We're just getting started." I had never had more than one drink in my life but decided to make an exception since it was Bernice's wedding.

Juan flashed his set of white teeth. "Let's go." We rose and made our way to the bartender.

"One more shot of the good stuff," he told the man, who reached down and grabbed it from below and poured us each a shot. Juan and I clinked glasses.

"To love and happiness," he said. "May we both have it the rest of our lives."

"I'll drink to that," I said, downing the elixir in one gulp.

Aunt Grace came to join us. She studied me, seeming satisfied with what she saw. "Looks like you've finally let loose. Good girl," she praised.

I smiled back at her, unsure how to respond. A fast song started, and Juan suggested we dance. Soon, we were next to Alejandro and Bernice. I did my best to copy Juan's dance moves, the booze seeming to have done wonders for my form.

Suddenly, just as Juan predicted, the night was over. Bernice and Alejandro said goodbye to everyone and headed to their hotel room. And I, drunk and sweaty, stumbled toward the nearby guest bedroom.

"Don't forget to say goodbye before you leave," Juan called after me. I promised I'd remember, and later, as I lay on my bed, I realized if things were different, I wouldn't go home.

Chapter 30

I woke up feeling like I'd been hit by a train. Every muscle in my body ached, and my head hurt so much it was unbearable. Finally, I forced myself out of bed to use the restroom, and on the way there, I reminded myself not to live it up like that ever again.

Grace found me on the way back to my room. "I made breakfast," she said in a soothing tone. "You should eat a little something before you leave."

"Thanks," I rasped. My voice sounded awful.

I padded to the kitchen and sat at the table. Bright light streamed in through the sheer curtains, making me cringe.

"Here," Grace said, handing me two aspirins. "This will help."

I wordlessly accepted them and dug into my meal. After eating half of it, I took the medication and checked the time. I had to hurry up and get ready because Bernice would be over in an hour to take me to the airport. I had told her not to since it was the day after her wedding, but she'd insisted. She wanted to be the one to take me and say goodbye.

After putting my hair up, I took a quick shower. The hot water felt so good I could have stood there all day. Instead, I was in and out in ten minutes. I managed to make myself look somewhat presentable, taking the remaining time to smash my belongings into the suitcase and snap it closed.

I heard Bernice pull up as I dragged my luggage to the foyer. The front door opened, and she smiled at me.

"You look amazing," I told her. "Your skin is glowing."

She grinned. "Wish I could say the same for you."

"It's Juan's fault," I joked. "Speaking of which, I promised I'd say goodbye before we left."

"Sure. Just let me put your suitcase in the car, and we'll head over there."

Juan came outside when we saw us coming.

"You don't even look hung over," I told him.

He smiled. "I'll take that as a compliment. The truth is, I feel like crap."

Bernice laughed, but I found myself feeling serious all of a sudden. "It was nice meeting you, Juan. Thanks for everything," I said. And I meant it too. I wouldn't have changed a thing. Every day in New Mexico had been a blast.

"Nice meeting you, too," he said. "Don't be a stranger."

"I won't." I wasn't sure if I should hug him goodbye or not, so instead, I simply chose to wave.

Bernice and I got in the car and headed to Albuquerque.

"So, how was it?" I asked.

Bernice took her eyes off the road to glance at me. "Amazing. I'm going to do it again when I get back home."

"I feel bad I took you away."

"Don't feel bad. I wanted to take you."

The scenery zipped past as we chatted, and as we got closer to town, I said, "I had so much fun. Jim would have loved it here." Once I said his name, I realized how much I missed him.

"Come together next time," she suggested.

We pulled into the airport and parked the car. She sat with me until it was time to board the plane.

"You'll visit Chicago, too," I said. "We're still going to see each other, right?"

Bernice's eyes filled with tears. "We're going to see each other plenty. I promise."

I hugged her and smiled, wiping some of my tears away. Then, I boarded the plane and fastened my seat belt. After the plane filled with passengers, I heard the engines roar, signaling we were ready for take-off. Once we were in the air, I gazed out the window, admiring the mountains one last time before closing my eyes and falling asleep.

Jim waved at me while smiling brightly as I walked off the plane. I ran to him and gave him a big hug and kiss.

"I missed you," he whispered in my ear.

"I missed you, too," I cooed.

We held hands on the way to get the luggage while I babbled non-stop about the wedding, going horseback riding, and drinking too much alcohol. Jim listened to it all.

Once we were heading home, he said, "Boy. I'm sorry I missed the wedding. It sounded like a great time."

The next day Jim and I brought dinner to his dad, who was feeling much better. The three of us spending time together reminded me I was happy with the life I had and that it didn't matter where I lived. I had everything I wanted. Well, almost everything. I thought of our reunion the night before and had no doubt I'd get pregnant soon.

I stopped by Jeannie's the next day. She wanted to hear about Bernice's wedding, so I filled her in on all the details. "Sounds like this Juan had the hots for you," she said.

"You think so? I don't know. Anyway, he knows I'm married."

Jeannie shrugged, then went to change Lisa's diaper. While she was gone, I wondered if Jim had gotten the same impression. I hoped not. I didn't want him to think he had something to worry about.

When Jeannie returned, we changed subjects and began chatting about Lisa. She filled me in on all the cute things she had done recently. We talked all afternoon, and as I was about to help her start dinner, Chuck came home, looking distraught.

"What is it, honey?" Jeannie asked him.

Chuck let out a heavy sigh. "I'm afraid I've got some bad news." He walked into the family room, said hello to me, then took a seat. "My buddy's younger brother died in Vietnam. He's completely devastated." Chuck glanced at me. "You might know him, Lou. He was your age. A kid named Frankie."

When Chuck said "Frankie," I burst into tears.

Jeannie scooted closer. "You okay?" she asked.

I nodded, still sobbing. I don't know what had come over me, but I couldn't stop crying.

Chuck left the room and returned with a box of Kleenex. I nodded thanks, took some, and blew my nose while they both sat in silence.

"I'm sorry," I said. "It just feels so odd to think of him gone. I mean, we weren't the best of friends – we were probably even enemies for a time – but we grew up together, you know?"

"Yeah," Chuck said, nodding. I made eye contact with him and wondered what unspeakable horrors he'd experienced over there. He had still never told anyone, not even Jeannie.

We spent the rest of the night reminiscing. I chose to discuss the good times I'd had with Frankie instead of the many disagreements, and by the time Jim came to pick me up, I was feeling a little bit better.

"I feel bad Frankie and I drifted apart," Jim said as we lay next to each other. He leaned over and gave me a kiss. "If it weren't for him, I wouldn't have met you."

"True." I thought of that day at the soda shop. Frankie had made me so angry with his silly prank, but I had forgiven him. We were young and did stupid things then.

Jim, Chuck, Jeannie, and I drove to the funeral together. No one uttered a word on the way there. I glanced at Jim as he drove. His hands gripped the steering wheel, and his jaw tensed. He had apologized in advance, saying he didn't do well at funerals and that he wouldn't be very pleasant today.

I smiled inside, knowing how hard it was for him to admit what he considered a weakness to me, and hoped I could find strength for the both of us.

Chuck found Frankie's Mom and Dad and offered his condolences. Jeannie stood at his side, nodding politely, not having known Frankie very well herself. After a few minutes of chatting, they moved on, and Jim and I approached.

"Sorry for your loss," Jim said to Frankie's dad.

The man nodded, doing his best to stay composed. "Thank you," he said.

I made eye contact with Frankie's mom and stepped forward. "Frankie and I grew up together," I told her. She smiled, her face brightening for a moment. "We didn't always see eye to eye, but as we got older, we became friends. I can't believe he's..." My voice cracked, and I couldn't go on. His dad got teary-eyed, and his mom reached for my hand and squeezed it. "I'm so sorry," I said, then Jim and I moved on, taking a seat next to Jeannie and Chuck.

I sat and listened to the pastor's prayers with closed eyes. Afterward, Frankie's mom got up to speak. She held a folded piece of paper. With visibly trembling hands, she opened it up.

"I'd like to say a few things about my son, Frank." She cleared her throat and stared out at the center of the crowd. "My son was a joy to be around. He made life worth living." She paused, trying to keep it together so she could finish.

I heard Jim sniffling next to me and reached for his hand.

"Frank was a caring person," his mom continued. "Especially to animals. He volunteered at the pound once a week, cleaning cages and brushing dogs' and cats' hair. He wanted to be a veterinarian and spent countless hours telling us of all the pets' lives he planned to save."

Tears ran down my face as I pictured Frankie, with his chubby freckled cheeks and unruly brown hair, working hard on a Sunday to make a difference in the lives of unwanted pets. I had never known that side of him. For most of my life, I had thought of him as a bully, bent on making my life a living hell.

"When he got older, he wanted to join the army and fight for his country. He wanted to do his part." She let out a heavy sigh. "I didn't want him to go. I was afraid if he left, I'd lose my son." She began to sob, and I chanced a glance at Chuck, who sat still as a statue, listening. "Before he left, he told me not to worry. He said he wasn't afraid of anything, not even death."

There wasn't a dry eye in the room when she finished her

speech. After the last prayer, we all rose and went to the casket to pay our final respects. I recognized many of the kids we had graduated with as they went up one by one. Then Chuck kneeled before him and cried while Jeannie watched the scene, heartbroken.

Jim went before me, said a short prayer, and left. Then I stepped forward.

"Hey, Frank," I whispered. "You look different." I studied him, trying to figure out why. "It's your face. It's thinner. Like a man's."

I smiled as a tear rolled down my cheek. "But you've still got the same freckles."

Chapter 31

A few years passed, and Jim and I still hadn't had a baby, despite going at it like rabbits. Jim didn't seem fazed by our predicament. I, on the other hand, had grown more discouraged each year.

"Come here," he said, taking my hand and leading me to the sofa.

I sat, wondering what was left to say.

Jim held my gaze, a loving expression on his face. "If you really want to be a parent, we can adopt," he said.

We hadn't discussed the possibility yet, but I had given it a lot of thought lately.

"I appreciate you being open to the idea, I really do, but I had hoped to have a child of my own...our child."

Jim nodded. "I understand. I'd like that, too. But I want you to know I'm happy, Lou. I don't need anyone but you."

His admission melted my heart. "That means a lot," I said, feeling my spirits lift.

Jim took my face in his hands and gently kissed my lips. When he pulled away, he said, "How about we never stop trying."

***

Bernice and I hadn't seen each other since the wedding but kept in touch every week by phone.

"So, what will you do now that you're done with school?" I asked her. I imagined the opportunities were endless with a business degree from UNM.

"I'm not sure," she said. "I'm tossing around a couple of ideas."

I stirred cake batter with one hand and held the phone to my ear with the other. "What's the best one?"

"Well, I'd like to get pregnant, for starters."

"That's a given."

"And I don't know if I've told you, but my aunt has been a little loopy lately. She's been forgetting things, so she asked me to take over her business affairs. You know, just the book royalties and other investments." She paused, then added, "I'll tell you what, she may be outspoken and eccentric, but she's managed to do all right financially."

I smiled, remembering how unusual Grace had been when we met.

"And I'd like to start my own business," Bernice said excitedly. "I was thinking maybe a jewelry store or an art gallery, but then I was thinking of opening a hot dog stand. What do you think?"

Memories of burnt taste buds resurfaced. "I think it's an excellent idea. You could get a little cart and offer Chicago-style hot dogs in Santa Fe!"

"Juan said we'd have to add green chile to them or they won't sell."

"He would say that," I smirked. "How's he been lately?"

"You mean since he stopped pining for you and married someone else? Pretty good. He's been busy running the ranch with Alejandro and his dad."

"Glad to hear he's doing well," I said. "But back to your business. You could offer a Chicago-style dog, and a spicier, local version. That way, everyone is happy. Seriously, I think it will be a big hit."

"I have a gut feeling this will be successful, and now that I hear you saying it, I know it will be."

"And who better to do it than you?" I added. "I'm excited. I can't wait to visit."

"You keep saying you and Jim are going to take a trip. When are you coming?"

"I'm working on it," I assured her. "He's just so busy with

the apartment buildings and now the Laundromat. It's hard for him to break away. He's even got me busy helping."

"Well, hurry up and come down. I want to be the one to serve you a Chicago dog."

***

That summer, everyone in the neighborhood was panicking as the police searched for serial killer Richard Speck. A lady from Mom's church knew one of the victims, a young nurse in the prime of her life who had been brutally murdered. Mom was so freaked out she decided to come over since Dad wasn't home.

"Screw that," Jeannie said as we talked on the phone. "I'm coming over, too."

Chuck dropped Jeannie and Lisa off on his lunch break. After he left, we sat in the living room, listening to Mom recount all the gruesome details she had read in the newspaper. When she finished, she said, "I wish they'd catch him already. This is so stressful."

My nerves were on edge, and as I glanced at Lisa, I was thankful she was only three years old and couldn't understand what was going on. Instead, she sat on the floor, happily playing with a stuffed animal, oblivious to the dangers of the real world.

I heard a loud clunk come from the bedroom.

"What was that?" Jeannie gasped.

"I don't know," I said. "Let me go check."

Mom looked concerned as I got up and crept toward the bedroom. I didn't see anyone but reached in the dresser drawer and pulled out the pistol Jim had taught me how to use just in case. Then, holding it firmly in my hand, I pushed the curtains aside and peered out the window.

A black crow sat on the windowsill. His beady eye met mine, and I sighed, realizing that we were just getting worked up by our discussion.

"It's just a bird," I called out, then put the gun away and

returned to the sofa.

It wasn't until the manhunt ended that any of us got quality sleep. Me especially, as stress triggered the nightmare of the Williams family fire. It seemed no matter how much time passed, they were on my mind, at least in my subconscious.

A few weeks later, Jim and I were on the sofa watching TV when the news came on. A newscaster I had never seen before began speaking, and I did a double-take when I saw his face.

"Isn't that Jeannie's old boyfriend, Tad?" Jim asked.

"Yeah. I think it is."

"He's decent," Jim said, then tossed a handful of popcorn in his mouth. He had been confused about why Jeannie dumped Tad and married Chuck soon afterward. My response had been to shrug and say when it came to matters of the heart, there was no logic, an answer he had accepted without question.

Jeannie was over the next week. "Can you believe it? Now I'm stuck seeing Tad every night."

"You don't have to watch him. You can change the channel," I suggested, thinking she was being overly dramatic.

Lisa grabbed a framed photo off the coffee table, and Jeannie snatched it from her before she dropped it on the ground.

"I've tried," she admitted. "But I feel compelled to watch, and the more I watch, the worse I feel."

"You can't let this eat you alive," I warned. "You made a choice, one you have to live with."

Jeannie stared at her lap.

"You did it so you could live a life with the man you love," I said.

Her expression remained unchanged.

"You have to stop watching the news on that channel," I said. "If you don't, you're going to drive yourself nuts."

"You're right," she said as she lifted her face. "I see Tad and then look over at Chuck, thinking about what I've done, and it's like they're both in the room, judging me."

My heart sank. Her happiness was all I had in mind when we'd discussed which choice to make. Now it seemed that very happiness eluded her because of the decision.

"I love you, Jean. I don't want to see you torturing yourself. Life is too short."

On her way out, I said, "Promise me you'll stop watching Tad on TV."

"I promise," she replied.

Bernice called the next day with the latest news about her business. "I just got my license, and the cart is on its way. I'm going to call it Chicago Dogs. What do you think?"

"It's perfect," I said. "The locals will love it."

"Well, the adventurous ones, anyway. I suspect hot dogs are as foreign to the locals as good Mexican food was to you!"

"Having second thoughts?"

"Not really. People love to talk about visiting big cities like Chicago, but they never go. This way, they can have a taste of the big city right in their back yard."

"That's brilliant! You are such a smart businesswoman."

We talked about what kind of chips she'd serve and which sodas she'd stock. Bernice was ecstatic and said she'd love to have a second location in Taos if it went well. I assured her it would be a big success.

After chatting about the details and me telling her about my week, she said, "Oh my gosh. I almost forgot to tell you the news. Juan's wife is pregnant!" she squealed. "I'm going to be an aunt."

I felt a pang of jealousy and chalked it up to being unable to conceive yet.

"That's wonderful," I said. "Tell him I said congratulations."

Chapter 32

Jeannie and I had planned a party for Lisa's fifth birthday but had to cancel at the last minute because she was sick. We both agreed it was terrible timing and decided to have a small get-together as soon as she felt better. The TV was blaring when I hung up the phone, and I was about to tell Jim to turn it down when I saw Tad delivering breaking news: "Dr. Martin Luther King, Jr. has been assassinated," he said.

Jim and I stayed up late talking about what happened, and when the phone rang the next morning, I was groggy.

"Sorry to call so early," Jeannie said. "The doctor had a cancellation and can fit Lisa in today, but Chuck already left for work."

"Jim's gone, too. He had to pick up a permit across town. How about I meet you at your place, and we'll take the bus to Lawndale together?" I suggested.

"Thanks so much, Lou. See you soon."

Lisa looked miserable on the ride over. Her eyelids were heavy, and her lower lip protruded as she rested her head against Jeannie's chest. Thankfully, the doctor was able to see her right away. I sat in the waiting room reading a magazine. They were gone longer than expected, and when they finally came out, Jeannie paid the bill, and we left.

I could have sworn I smelled smoke when we stepped outside and was just about to ask Jeannie if she smelled it too when I heard a loud crash in the distance. I turned to see what was happening and saw a group of young black men coming down the street, shouting and throwing rocks through windows.

"Oh, shit!" I said.

Jeannie and I made eye contact, and without speaking, she

scooped Lisa into her arms, and we began running as fast as we could in the opposite direction.

"Where's the bus?" she asked, frantic.

I squinted down the street but didn't see one coming.

"Turn here," I shouted as we approached the corner.

We ran down the next block, scanning from left to right, in search of help as more windows broke and the voices of the angry mob grew louder. Several cars zoomed past. Jeannie and I tried to flag them down to no avail, so we kept running.

Sirens wailed in the distance as thick smoke filled the air. Buildings were set on fire, one by one, and the next thing I knew, there was another group of angry rioters coming from the other direction.

A bus sped up the street, and Jeannie practically ran out in front of it.

"I have a child!" she shouted. "Stop!"

The bus slowed but didn't stop as the driver opened the door so we could hop on. Jeannie lost her balance on the way up and accidentally bumped Lisa's head against the railing, causing her to start crying. Once Jeannie righted herself, she rubbed Lisa's forehead to comfort her. A rock shattered the bus window, and the few passengers on board began to scream.

"Get down!" the bus driver yelled.

Jeannie and I dropped to the ground, using our bodies to shield Lisa. The driver made a sharp right, and we slid across the floor, finally coming to a stop when he began driving straight again. The driver was clearly improvising, turning wherever he could find an opening in the chaos to make it to safety.

There was an explosion outside, and people began shouting. I closed my eyes, memories of the Williams fire resurfacing, and all of a sudden, I couldn't breathe. It took everything I had to keep it together in front of Jeannie and Lisa as the bus careened from left to right.

After what felt like an eternity, we came to an abrupt stop.

The remaining passengers were so anxious to get off they trampled over us. After everyone had gone, I pulled myself up and looked around. Jeannie rose, looking disoriented, and grabbed Lisa, who had gone silent since the explosion, and we got off the bus.

The city's sky glowed orange through the haze as it burned out of control, making it hard to figure out where we were. Luckily, the driver had taken us to a less turbulent spot, and I scanned the area for a payphone.

"There," I pointed. "On the corner." We ran toward it as fast as we could.

I dug through my purse for a coin and grabbed the receiver. Then, with shaky hands, I called home.

"Jim!" I rejoiced when he answered.

"Lou. Where are you?" he asked, panicked.

I had no idea. Thankfully, Jeannie could make out the names of the cross streets and told me.

"I know where that is," he said. "Stay put. I'll be right there."

Adrenalin coursed through my veins as we waited for Jim, my eyes darting to and fro, looking for rioters. The hysteria turned to an eerie calm, and I heard the familiar rumble of Jim's engine. When I saw his car, I was shocked. It looked like it had been through a war zone.

He stopped, and we climbed in, slamming the doors shut before he peeled out.

"You okay?" he asked, stealing a glance at me.

"I think so."

As Jim negotiated the side streets, I slumped in my seat, exhausted and numb. I watched the neighborhood go by as if in slow motion, and although there was activity, I couldn't hear a sound.

Chuck was waiting outside when we got home. When he saw Jeannie and Lisa, he rushed to them.

"Thank God you're safe." He sobbed as he hugged them tightly.

I stared blank-faced, feeling like I was watching a scene in a movie.

Chuck released them, and we wordlessly nodded at each other before they got in their car and left.

Jim looked me up and down after we went inside, his expression pained. "You're in one piece," he said in a soft voice. "But you've got footprints on your back."

Hearing that made me burst into tears.

"Come here," he said, pulling me close. He held me in his arms and let me sob. And instead of asking me a bunch of questions, he just rubbed my back, the way my parents used to when I was a little kid.

"Let's get you cleaned up," he said when I had finally finished crying and led me by the hand to the bathroom.

I scrubbed myself clean, leaning back and putting my feet on the edge of the tub. I stared at my big toe until the water turned cold, then got out, put on pajamas, and went to bed. The next morning, I woke to the smell of breakfast and went to find Jim.

"Morning," he said.

I shuffled over and gave him a kiss.

"How are you feeling?"

"Sore. Like someone walked on top of me."

"That's not funny."

"I know." I pulled out a chair and took a seat.

"You wanna talk about it?" he asked.

I sighed. "I don't think so. At least not right now."

We ate and then turned on the TV to hear the latest: "Thousands of police officers were unable to control the violence, so the Illinois National Guard has been deployed to assist them in stopping the arsonists and looters. Proving he's not taking the situation lightly, Mayor Daley has given police authority to shoot to kill any arsonist or anyone with a Molotov cocktail in their hand and shoot to maim or cripple any looters."

Jim lowered the volume. "Let's go back to bed," he said.

Newscasters had advised people to stay indoors, so we spent the day at home, trying to catch up on much-needed rest. I called Jeannie in the evening to see how she was doing, then asked if I could speak to Lisa.

"Hey, honey. How are you feeling?" I asked when she answered.

"Better," she said in a sweet but small voice.

"Happy Birthday," I said. "Sorry we're not having the party, but your mom says we're going to dinner at Grandma and Grandpa's house soon. She's going to make your favorite cake, and you're going to get presents."

"Okay," she replied.

Jeannie came on the line, and we talked for a little longer about how the world had gone crazy overnight and how dangerous life could be, then we hung up, saying we'd see each other soon.

A week later, we all sat around my parent's dinner table talking about the riots. "Your car looks like hell," Dad said to Jim. "What a shame."

"I know. I'll have to stop by Chuck's and have it repaired." Jim shook his head and sighed. "I went to the South Side for a permit, and let's just say it was a case of wrong place, wrong time." He hadn't elaborated, but I assumed his experience was similar to ours.

Jeannie and I eyed each other. "I know the feeling," I said. "Jeannie and I were running down streets with Lisa in tow as rioters were breaking windows and setting buildings on fire. Luckily, Jeannie saw a bus and ran out in front of it. She made the driver stop, otherwise who knows what would have happened to us?"

"Then things got crazier when our bus was attacked, and our driver took some shortcuts to bring us all to safety," Jeannie added.

Lisa looked up. "That's when the people stepped on Aunt Lou."

Everyone turned to me, shocked, but I just shrugged it off.

"They sure were in a hurry, huh?" I said to Lisa and went to get the cake off the counter and put it on the table. Dad lit the candles, and Jim dimmed the lights, and everyone sang Happy Birthday.

Chapter 33

Before I knew it, we were celebrating Lisa's 18th birthday. It seemed like just yesterday she was a little girl, and Jeannie and I were running with her through the streets of Chicago, trying to escape the riots.

Today, we were headed to the Walnut Room. Just Lisa, Jeannie, and me. We'd taken her once before when she was ten, and when I asked her if she'd like to eat anywhere special for her birthday, she said she wanted to return.

Jeannie's doorbell wasn't working, so I knocked instead.

"Ouch!" I cried out, surprised by the sharp shooting pain in my knuckle. A moment later, Lisa answered.

"Happy Birthday!" I said cheerily, ignoring the discomfort.

"Thanks," she said, giving me a hug.

Jeannie and I had suggested taking the train downtown, but Lisa claimed to enjoy driving in the city, and since it was her day, I let her drive my car.

Lisa weaved in and out of the congestion with ease, then squeezed the sedan into a spot so small it was hard to believe it could fit.

"How did you do that?" Jeannie asked when we got out.

"Dad taught me." Lisa grinned.

The relationship Lisa had with Chuck was special. She went out of her way to pay attention when he showed her things like how to change a tire or the basics of hand to hand combat for self-defense, and he went out of his way to appear genuinely interested in accompanying her and Jeannie when they did things like shop for a prom dress and matching shoes.

As the years passed, I was confident Jeannie had made the right decision, however immoral it may have been. And once she had heard Tad married a Chicago socialite and started a family of his own, her inner struggle with guilt finally dissipated.

The waiter handed us the menus. Lisa lifted hers, scanned it, and quickly set it down. "We're supposed to have the pot pie, right?"

"Have whatever you like. Everything is good," I promised. I'd never ordered anything but the pot pie but knew the rest of the food measured up based on the restaurant's reputation.

Lisa picked the menu back up and perused its offerings a second time. "I think I'll stick with pot pie," she reiterated, then set the menu down again.

I smiled at her. She was so grown up and beautiful, with naturally wavy blonde hair and bright blue eyes. Her skin glowed with health, something mine hadn't done in a while. My eyelids sagged slightly, and my cheeks were a little lower, making me look perpetually tired.

The truth was I did feel tired all the time. I attributed it to getting older.

The waiter returned to take our order, interrupting my thought. When he left, I looked directly at Jeannie. She nodded, and I turned to Lisa.

"Jim and I have a special birthday present for you."

Lisa seemed excited to find out what we had gotten her but looked confused since I wasn't holding anything.

"We heard you talking about how you missed your friends who had moved to the suburbs and how hard it was to get to see them, so...we're buying you a car."

"Oh my God!" Lisa gasped. She practically jumped from her seat. "I don't know what to say. It's just so...it's amazing. Thanks so much! Tell Uncle Jim I said thank you, too."

The happy look on her face made it worth every penny. Jim and I never managed to have kids of our own. We didn't adopt, either. Instead, we chose to spoil Lisa every chance we got.

"Here's the plan," I said. "You and your dad are going to shop for a car together. And once you've found the one you like that he says is in great condition and is within the price range we've discussed, Jim and I will go there and pay for it." I wanted to buy Lisa a brand new car, but Jeannie wouldn't have it, so we agreed to find one a couple of years old with low miles.

Our food arrived, and after I dug in, I blew on the steamy forkful, remembering my first visit to the restaurant with Bernice. I still had the nightgown she gave me and wore it every year on my wedding anniversary.

"What are you thinking about?" Jeannie asked, noticing the change in my expression.

She was always so good at reading me. "I'm thinking about the first time I ate here with Bernice."

"Isn't that your friend from New Mexico?" Lisa asked, placing her napkin in her lap.

"It is. You didn't get to meet her last time she was here, but she's coming back soon, and I'm hoping we can all do something fun together."

Bernice had come to Chicago a few times since her wedding, which I was grateful for since Jim and I never made it to New Mexico. I had hoped he and I would take romantic trips to Europe or somewhere tropical since we could afford it, but he never seemed to be able to break away.

"Didn't you say they were all coming this time?" Jeannie asked.

"Yeah. Bernice is bringing the whole crew. Alejandro and her two sons, Jeffrey and Eric." Bernice had her first child after her business took off. Chicago Dogs was so popular she had one in Taos, several in Albuquerque, and had sold franchises to people in Scottsdale and Tucson, Arizona.

"I can babysit if you want," Jeannie offered. "That way you two can have a night to yourselves."

Bernice had told me the boys were a handful, one aged eleven and one nine.

"I'm sure we'll be taking you up on that offer."

Jeannie was great with kids, the proof sitting opposite me. I smiled at Lisa. "You're still going to go to school for that new thing, right?" I asked.

"Computers," she said. Lisa had said they were the future.

"What exactly will you do with them?"

"I'm going to learn programming."

"Programming," I repeated. I had no idea what she meant, but she seemed excited about her chosen profession, which made me happy.

The waiter came with the check a moment later, and Jeannie grabbed it. She insisted on treating since Jim and I were buying her daughter such an expensive gift.

I woke the next day feeling exhausted. And my knuckle still hurt. I opened my eyes and inspected it closer. It was swollen and red, which I thought was odd because all I had done was knock on Jeannie's front door.

I ignored it, got up and showered, and went on with my day. I had plans to meet Jim for lunch after I scheduled appointments for a few tenants who had issues in need of repair. We liked to get problems taken care of right away, treating the people who rented from us like we would want to be treated, and in return, most were kind and paid their rent on time.

The day after that, I woke up feeling like someone had beaten me in my sleep. It reminded me of how I felt the day after I got trampled in the riots. Only now, I had a hard time breathing, and the pain in my knuckle had spread to the surrounding knuckles, and my wrist was swollen.

I stayed in bed the rest of the week. I told Jim I had the flu and hoped I'd start feeling better soon so I could get on with my life. Jim was sweet and doted on me, bringing me chicken soup from the corner restaurant and spending extra time at home. When I hadn't improved after a few days, he suggested I see a doctor. Not being a fan of physicians, I forced myself out of bed and pretended to be okay.

Jim and I were at my parent's house the following week for dinner when my dad asked, "What's the matter, honey? You look miserable."

I thought I was doing a good job of hiding how I felt, but my dad was too observant.

"I'm fine," I lied. "Why?"

"I don't know. You just seem irritable."

He was right. I was irritable. Something about feeling like crap for two weeks did that to me.

I sighed. "I haven't been feeling so hot lately. I guess it shows."

We sat around the table chatting, and as we ate dessert, my mom asked me what symptoms I had. I told her while showing her my wrist and hand. She looked alarmed and exchanged a look with my dad but didn't say anything.

"You're going to the doctor," Jim said on the way home. "That's not a request."

I felt like a child who had just been scolded. Jim rarely put his foot down, but when he did, it was final.

Dragging my feet, I went to the scheduled appointment. The doctor asked me a bunch of questions, then took my temperature and pulse and listened to my lungs. He pulled out a needle.

"This won't hurt. We just need to run some blood tests."

I nodded and turned my head as I felt my skin pinch. When I got home, I had a bruise that seemed to grow larger and uglier by the hour. It hadn't even gone away by the time I went back the next week to find out the test results.

It wasn't the flu. It was rheumatoid arthritis. And it wasn't going to go away.

Chapter 34

Jim had been trying to cheer me up for weeks since the doctor gave me the bad news. As we lay in bed one night, he snuggled up to me.

"At least it's not something deadly, like cancer," he said in an optimistic tone.

He was right. I wasn't dying. Just losing my capacity to enjoy life bit by bit, day by day. Something no one could understand unless they'd experienced it. Sadly, it had only been a couple of months, and I'd already had enough.

"And there's always new medicines," he added. "They'll find a cure. You'll see."

Jim had been bending over backward to be as helpful as possible. From opening jars to carrying grocery bags, he was really going out of his way, for which I was grateful. I just didn't like feeling helpless. I liked to do things for him, to feel needed, not the other way around.

My mom stopped by to visit. She had been trying to baby me whenever she could, too. Today she kept hovering. She watched as I struggled with the can opener.

"You want me to do that?" she asked.

"No," I snapped, then set the can opener down and let out a heavy sigh. "Sorry, Mom. I didn't mean that. It's just lately everyone has been treating me like I'm an invalid, and it's frustrating."

Mom came over and put her hand on my shoulder. "No one thinks you're an invalid, honey. We just want to help."

A solitary tear escaped my eye. The first one I had cried since learning the news from the doctor. "I know."

She gave me a big hug. When she let go, I stepped aside and let her open the can. I was embarrassed that a person older than me — my own mother — had to assist me with such a simple task. Suddenly, I couldn't wait to go back to the doctor and discuss medications. I had been putting off doing that, hoping if I ignored the situation, it would go away.

Newly motivated, I set up a follow-up appointment with the doctor. He suggested a steroid for the quickest relief, and after taking it, I felt like my old self again. Soon, I was back to checking on tenants, dealing with business paperwork, and cooking and cleaning without anyone's help.

I got home from the hair salon, and Jim told me Bernice had called. I called her back, figuring she wanted to discuss where to take the kids when she came to visit.

"Change of plans," she told me. "We aren't coming to visit now."

"Why not?" I asked.

"There have been some problems here, and Alejandro thinks it's best if we stay behind. We had hoped to visit everyone and do some business with our vendor, but it's just not a good time."

"Is everything okay with you and Alejandro?"

"Yeah. We're fine. The issue is with Juan." Bernice didn't elaborate.

"I'm sorry to hear that," I said.

"Juan was actually thinking of coming to Chicago instead. To meet with the sales rep and do some sightseeing."

I didn't know what to say.

"What do you think?" she asked, breaking the awkward silence.

"I... I think that sounds like a great idea. I'd be happy to show him the sights."

"Thanks, Lou. I really appreciate it. It would only be one day on the weekend. The other day he's going to be working."

"No problem," I said. I hung up the phone, hoping it wouldn't cause a problem with Jim.

I explained the situation to him. "He doesn't need a ride from the airport. He just needs someone to take him sightseeing." Jim looked like he had mixed feelings about it. "You wanna come with us? We could go to the Sears Tower, see all the tourist spots."

"No. You take him. You're good at cheering people up," he said, smiling. "Plus, I don't even know the guy."

I barely knew him myself. I was a little nervous about meeting again, wondering what we'd talk about.

A few days later, when I walked into the restaurant where we'd agreed to meet, Juan flashed me a big smile. It was warm and genuine and made me relax instantly.

"Welcome to the big city!" I said.

"Thanks. I'm glad I finally made it here. Took me long enough, huh?"

The hostess seated us, and we sat opposite each other. It was true I didn't know Juan well, but what I did remember was he had a spirit that was larger than life. That spirit seemed to have faded.

"So, how've you been?" I asked.

He exhaled loudly. "I'm getting a divorce."

"I'm sorry to hear that. That's got to be hard."

"It is. I never saw it coming."

The waiter came and took our order. We both got steaks. I ordered a soda, and Juan chose a glass of wine.

"You wanna talk about it?" I asked.

The drinks arrived, and Juan took a big sip of his wine. "Where to begin? My wife, Carla, had bought a couple of paintings from a local gallery..." He paused. "No. I shouldn't burden you with my story of woe."

"You don't have to tell me if you don't want to...but it's fine if you do. Sometimes it's good to talk about difficult things."

He nodded, a sad smile on his face. "Okay. But stop me anytime. I don't want to turn this visit into a counseling session. We're supposed to be enjoying the city."

"And we will." I nodded at him. "Go on."

"Well, Carla got interested in going to the art showings on

Friday nights. There's a bunch of them scheduled all the time. We went to a few showings together, but it just wasn't my thing, so I suggested she go with her girlfriends."

I had a pretty good idea where this was going but didn't say anything.

"So a little time passed, and I noticed she wasn't interested in me that way anymore." Juan averted his eyes. He took another sip of his drink. "Turns out she was screwing around with another guy. Some Dutch artist."

The food arrived, pausing the conversation. After the waiter left, we continued.

"How did you find out?"

Juan cut into his steak. "I had been suspicious because of her actions and some of the things she said. I asked around, talked to a few mutual friends. None of them wanted to directly accuse her of anything, but they had said enough. When it was clear she was having an affair, I decided to follow her one night."

I chewed my food. My neck muscles tensed as I listened.

"She went to a studio on Canyon Road, and after slipping in, closed the door but forgot to lock it. Curious, but filled with dread, I snuck in. There was classical music playing, and as I inched closer, trying to be quiet, I heard heavy breathing. Unable to stop myself, I stepped forward and saw a blond-haired guy having sex with my wife."

Juan wiped a tear from his eye. "I stood there listening to her moan and felt a part of my soul die."

I was speechless. I hadn't expected him to share in that much detail.

"I'm so sorry." I couldn't imagine how terrible he must feel.

"No...I'm sorry," he said. "I didn't mean to say so much."

Our waiter passed, and I flagged him down. "We'd like a bottle of wine, please. Whatever he was drinking."

The man nodded and went to fetch the much-needed booze.

Juan shook his head. "I really don't know why I told you all that. I haven't told that story to anyone."

"Maybe you just needed to get it off your chest."

The waiter arrived with the bottle of wine. He poured us each a glass, and I lifted mine. "You know we're drinking today, right?"

Juan found a smile. "Right. I can sleep off the hangover on the plane."

We clinked glasses, then spent the afternoon talking about happier things: the deal he just made to open a Chicago Dogs in California, his two daughters, Monica and Sylvia, whom he clearly adored.

"All I've been doing is talking about me all day. How's life been treating you?" Juan asked.

I thought about it for a while before answering. I wanted to make sure what I said was sincere. "I wanted to have a baby, but it never happened. But I'm okay with that because I have a niece named Lisa, who I love very much."

Juan smiled.

"I was recently diagnosed with rheumatoid arthritis, and although initially frustrated, I have it under control. I still get tired from time to time, but my husband Jim is always there to help."

"I'm glad he treats you right," Juan said, holding my gaze.

"Me, too," I said, then finished the last sip of my wine.

The waiter came with our check, and Juan paid the bill. We both rose and headed outdoors. It was a warm summer day, perfect for seeing the sights.

"Where to next?" I asked him. "We could go to the Sears Tower, and there's a ton of great museums. It's your vacation, so I'll let you decide."

Juan looked conflicted. "I think I'll pass on all of the above," he said. "I've already seen everything I came here for."

He gave me a warm smile. "Take care, Lou. And thanks for cheering me up."

"Anytime." I smiled.

Juan waved, then walked away. I watched him until he eventually disappeared into the sea of pedestrians, and I couldn't deny that there was something between us.

Chemistry.

I prayed he would find happiness with someone else someday.

Chapter 35

I left the nail salon in time to get home and rest for a while before Lisa's wedding. My manicure turned out great. The only ugly part was my crooked hands. They weren't as gnarled as Aunt Violet's had been, but they didn't look normal either. Definitely not the way a forty-seven-year-old woman's hands should look. Even though I took the newest drugs that stopped joint deterioration, they couldn't undo the damage that had already been done.

I frowned as I styled my hair, having myself a mini pity party.

"You look nice," Jim said as he gave me a peck on the cheek.

He had never stopped complimenting me. Even after I gained weight from the steroids, and even after my hands became slightly deformed. He always found ways to try and make me feel beautiful. When I said my fingers were hideous, he bought me a ring, saying they just needed proper decoration. When I couldn't fit into the nightgown Bernice had given me for our wedding, he bought a newer, prettier one in the correct size.

When I was too tired to keep up with everyone else, he'd say he was bushed too and suggest staying in for the evening. I felt guilty sometimes for holding him back. He was stuck with a wife who had the energy level of an elderly woman. "There's nowhere I'd rather be than with you," he'd say, and as I watched him now, standing in the mirror adjusting his tie, I thanked God for giving me such an amazing spouse. Disease or no disease, I was one lucky woman.

I hoped the man Lisa was marrying was just as wonderful.

"You have the card?" Jim asked on the ride over.

I held it up. My body might be a mess, but my mind was as

sharp as ever.

Lisa and Tim both had good jobs, but they had a lot of bills. With student loans, a mortgage, and two car payments, there wasn't much left over to go on the honeymoon Lisa really wanted, so Jim and I arranged the trip as a surprise.

"You think they're going to have a good time?" Jim asked, smiling warmly.

"She's always wanted to go to Tuscany."

Jim took my hand in his. "We're next," he said. "We should have done it sooner."

After years of being so focused on the business, Jim was finally beginning to realize life wasn't all about getting ahead and making money. We resolved together to start making time to really live.

Now we just had to wait until I felt better. I had been in a lot of pain lately but was going to see a new doctor, the best rheumatologist in the Midwest. If I was ever going to visit Europe, he would have to develop a pain management plan that allowed me to walk cobblestone streets all day.

Jim and I took a seat in the front pew next to Jeannie, my mom, and dad. When Lisa walked down the aisle with Chuck, she radiated happiness, and he beamed with pride. I stole a glance at Jeannie, who was already sniffling, and we smiled, sharing an unspoken communication only she and I knew.

As Lisa and Tim exchanged vows, I hung on their every word. I felt like I was watching my own daughter get married, and in a lot of ways, she was like my own daughter, thanks to my sister's generosity in sharing her with me.

Jeannie and I sat next to each other after dinner. "I'm stuffed," she said.

"Me too. I could fall asleep."

Just then, an Elvis song came on. Not just any Elvis song, but *It's Now or Never*. Jim got up, eager to dance with me, and although my feet were hurting, I laced my arms around his neck and slowly swayed from side to side, all while smiling as if I wasn't in any kind of pain.

I had gotten good at that out of necessity. It wasn't like I could complain about my symptoms all the time. If I did, no one would want to be around me. So I wore a happy face no matter how I felt. There were always two halves of me: the half who was truly enjoying myself and the half who suffered through. Then, of course, there were those rare days when I felt great, when the stars aligned and the moon was auspicious, but they were few and far between. When one of them did show up, I was so thrilled I wanted to do a million things, to enjoy every moment before it slipped away.

Jeannie took a sip of her cocktail and studied me as I sat back down.

"You put on a good show," she said.

"But I can never fool you." I slipped off my heels. "I should have worn flats."

"Why don't you dance barefoot?" she suggested. "No one would mind."

There wasn't a chance I would dance barefoot at a wedding, no matter how tempting the idea. "I think I'll just rest for a while," I said and spent the next few songs watching Lisa and Tim dance with Jeannie and Chuck.

Jim had been chatting with my parents by the bar but came and sat down next to me.

"How are you holding up?" he asked.

"I'm holding," I teased. "But seriously, this has been the best wedding. Once Lisa is free, let's pull her aside and give her the card."

"Okay," he said and scanned the room for her.

Wedding gifts were stacked on a table surrounding a special basket that held cards. We had kept our card in my purse because we wanted to give it to her in private. When I saw Jim on his way back with Lisa, I fished it out of my handbag and stood, fighting the grimace that the simple action demanded from me.

"This is for you," I told her. "We wanted to watch you open it."

Lisa took the card and held it in her hands for a beat before carefully pulling apart the seam. Inside were airline tickets, which she pulled out and squinted to read in the dim light. Lisa looked from Jim to me, wide-eyed and jaw agape. "This is incredible. I'm speechless. Thank you, guys. Thank you so much."

She wrapped her arms around me and gave me a hug. I closed my eyes, picturing her and her new hubby in the Italian countryside. The brief daydream morphed into a picture of Jim and me instead. I choked back a tear. "You're welcome, sweetie. Have a good time."

She thanked Jim again and put the card back in the envelope. "Wait until I tell Tim. He's going to flip!"

Lisa pranced away to find him. Jim smiled, then turned to me. "How about we head home? I'm kind of tired."

"You're always so tired," I said, a half-smile coming to my lips. "What am I going to do with you?"

"Just lie in bed with me while we look at travel brochures."

***

I called Bernice on Christmas Eve. "I can't believe the boys are grown. Where has the time gone?"

"I don't know. Jeff is twenty, and Eric is eighteen. I blink decades now," she joked.

I smiled, but it wasn't funny. I had missed her through the years and wished I could have spent more time with her and the kids.

"How's Juan doing?" I asked. Bernice had mentioned he had remarried the last time we talked.

"He's good. They just came back from a week in Europe. Alejandro and I watched the kids while they were gone, although they're older and they're girls, so they didn't need much watching."

I thought of Jeannie and me when we were young and smirked. We got into our fair share of trouble.

"Jim and I are planning a trip to Tuscany. You know, the one we always planned to take. We should take a girl's trip afterward. You, me, and Jeannie. What do you think?"

"Count me in," she said. "I could break away for a week."

"You serious?"

"Definitely. We should have done it ages ago."

"You're right. Why don't you pick some places, and I'll talk to Jeannie. Is next summer good?"

"Next summer is perfect. Now that the boys are working with Juan and Alejandro, I don't have to be as involved with the business on a day-to-day basis."

After I hung up, I couldn't wait to talk to Jeannie. Unfortunately, it was too late to call, but we would see each other the next day at Mom and Dad's.

When we had finished eating and opening gifts, I told Jeannie the plan.

"Sounds great. I'll just have to see if I can afford it," she said.

"Don't worry about the price. This one's on me," I said.

Jeannie had been okay with me spoiling Lisa but would never let me pay her way. I had learned to choose my battles wisely, though, and decided if she couldn't afford the vacation, I'd put up a fight this time. There was no way I would let anything get in the way of this trip.

Jeannie didn't have a passport, so we decided to get that taken care of first since we weren't sure where we were headed. I thought we should go somewhere tropical and spent the next few days mulling over Cancun and wanted Jeannie's opinion. I called her but kept getting the answering machine. She didn't return my calls.

Frustrated, I stopped by, unannounced. "Where have you been?" I asked.

"I've been around. I just haven't been feeling well."

"What's the matter?" I had been lecturing her about taking supplements. I found a few that had helped me and thought she should take them too.

She looked down.

"What's wrong?" I pressed.

Jeannie lifted her head, tears streaming down her face. "I'm dying, Lou. I have cancer."

Chapter 36

Over the next few months, our family went into a tailspin. Mom and Dad were trying to figure out how Jeannie could have gotten lung cancer when she had never smoked a cigarette in her life, and Chuck, a heavy smoker, blamed himself, assuming she had gotten ill because of him. Lisa was in a state of denial, believing the doctors would make her better, and I, after crying non-stop for several days, had re-emerged more motivated than ever to try and solve the problem.

I parked in the hospital lot and took a deep breath. Then I put on my happy face, something I had mastered long ago, before heading to Jeannie's room. She was sleeping when I arrived, so I stood by her side and studied her. She looked thinner than the day before and had lost a little more hair. Instead of improving, she seemed to be going downhill fast.

The reality of the situation hit home, and all of a sudden, I couldn't breathe. I slipped out the door and found refuge in the hallway bathroom, where I broke down and cried in a closed stall. A memory of Jeannie and me playing in the park surfaced, and I remembered our silly pact.

"Are you okay in there?" A woman asked, interrupting my thoughts.

I sniffled and wiped my nose with a wad of toilet paper. "I'm all right."

I opened the door and came face to face with Jeannie's doctor. When she saw who it was, her face fell.

"Hey, Lou. This is a tough time, I know." She reached for a proper tissue and offered it to me.

"Thanks." I blew my nose. There was a heavy silence, then I asked, "Isn't there anything more that can be done? I mean, they're always coming out with new medications, right?"

Jeannie's doctor sighed. "I'm afraid all we can do is make her comfortable at this point."

We had already had this discussion, where she explained to me that Jeannie's cancer was too advanced. She had even been kind to me when I had lost my patience with her. Now she was giving it to me straight again.

When she left, I splashed my face with cold water then touched up my makeup so it wouldn't look like I had been crying. Then, I took a few more deep breaths and tried to relax before going back to Jeannie's room.

Jeannie was awake when I returned. "Hey," she said in a soft voice. "Why so blue?"

I tried to smile but couldn't. "You know why," I said, holding her gaze.

She locked eyes with me, hers turning glassy. "You can't solve this one, Lou."

"I know," I said, choking back tears. "But this isn't how it was supposed to be."

Jeannie reached for my hand. "I was supposed to help you go at eighty. I remember. But it looks like plans have changed."

I sobbed uncontrollably. "But I can't do it without you."

"Then don't."

"What do you mean?"

Jeannie smiled at me. "I mean live, Lou. Live as long as you can...for me."

When we got the call in the middle of the night saying Jeannie had passed, I collapsed. It seemed like she had just told me yesterday she was ill, and now she was gone.

Bernice flew into town as soon as she heard what happened and offered to help Jim with the funeral arrangements. Ordinarily, I would have said no, but considering that my niece and her father were hysterical, my parents were in their late seventies and had been needing help themselves lately, and I was emotionally exhausted and suffering from a rheumatic flare, I willingly let her get involved.

I sat on the sofa, staring into space. I couldn't believe Jeannie was gone.

"That's all she does," I heard Jim say to Bernice from the other room. "I'm really worried."

"Me, too," she said.

I had taken medication to help me relax, and as I listened to them make phone calls and discuss where to have the luncheon, their voices sounded far away. I woke up in the same spot the next day, still wearing my clothes but covered by a blanket.

Bernice poked her head in. "You hungry?" she asked. "There's half an omelet I can heat up."

I couldn't remember the last time I had eaten. The medication made me foggy, and the days were a blur.

"I'll heat it," I said as I rose.

Every decrepit bone in my body creaked on the way to the kitchen, and as I walked there, I wondered if Bernice could hear the sounds, too.

"Thanks so much for coming here and helping out," I told her again as I turned on the burner.

"No problem. I just wish it wasn't for this reason."

She didn't have to say the rest. We had been anticipating taking a fantastic trip together, not planning my kid sister's funeral. I flipped the omelet and heated the other side, slid it onto a plate, and flopped in a chair.

Bernice sat down next to me. "Jim and I took care of everything. He said you two will swing by your parents and pick them up tomorrow."

"Aren't you coming with us?"

"No. I'm going to be driving with my parents. They said they wanted to be there for you."

They hardly knew Jeannie but had always been like family to me.

"I appreciate that," I said.

Bernice headed to her parent's house for the rest of the day. While I was alone, I picked up a pen and pad of paper and thought about what I might say at Jeannie's funeral. When Jim came home, he sat next to me and gave me a kiss on the cheek.

"What are you writing?" he asked.

"Something for tomorrow."

We both glanced at the blank sheet of paper. Hours had passed, and I hadn't written a single word.

"Why don't you take a break from this project," he said. "I brought pizza. Let's have some and turn in early."

Jim had dark circles under his eyes. I had been so busy grieving I hadn't seen he was suffering, too.

I took his hand. "I'm glad you're home. I love you so much."

His weary expression brightened. "I love you, too," he said, then pulled me close and gave me a hug.

I found it difficult to get out of bed the following day. I wasn't ready for what was to come – mentally or physically – and had to move in slow motion all the way to the shower. The hot spray helped ease some of the pain in my neck and shoulders, and when I got out, I popped a painkiller with a cup of coffee.

As I dressed, I realized I hadn't written anything for the service, which was probably just as well because I couldn't see myself being able to stand up and speak anyway.

We passed the old oak tree Jeannie and I used to climb, and my thoughts turned to my parents. I would have to make a point to spend as much time as I could with them now. I could only imagine the pain they must be experiencing after losing their youngest child.

It should've been me, I thought.

Jim parallel parked in front of my parents' house. I was so tired that it was a Herculean effort to make it from the car to the front door. My dad answered, looking worse than I did and much more frail.

"Hey, Dad," I said, hugging him. He gripped me tighter than he ever had, proving that although he appeared weak, he wasn't.

He held me for so long I thought he might never let go. When he did, I asked. "You ready?"

He nodded and took hold of my hand. Mom and I made eye contact as Jim interlaced his arm with hers, and they walked down the steps together. When we got to the car, I suggested Dad sit in front with Jim so I could be next to my mom. Since no one had anything to say, Jim turned on an easy listening channel to fill the heavy silence.

Lisa, Tim, Chuck, and Chuck's dad had just arrived when we got to the funeral home. Chuck approached me, and as he walked over, it seemed he had shrunk a few inches.

"How are you doing with the patch?" I asked. He had tried to quit smoking the day Jeannie was diagnosed but had been sneaking cigarettes in the backyard. Lisa had busted him and given him quite a lecture.

"Five days now," he replied, patting his upper arm.

Lisa looked miffed, so I dropped the subject. Instead, I went over and gave her a big hug, unsure what to say.

We all went inside. I saw Bernice and her parents and went over and said hello to them before taking a seat. I scanned the room, ignoring the coffin holding my sister front and center, and noticed some of Chuck's co-workers had shown up, along with a few neighbors Jeannie had made friends with.

The service began with a prayer, and then Chuck got up to speak.

"Most people don't know this," he said. "But I fell in love with Jeannie years before we started dating." He was reading from a piece of paper but paused to glance at me. "She had come to the shop with her father to have his car repaired, and even though she was too young to date at the time, I knew she was the one." Mom and Dad exchanged a look, and then he continued. "I had hoped to have a chance with her someday but ended up going to Vietnam instead." He paused. "I won't go into all that, but let's just say hoping I might see Jeannie again was one of the main things that kept me going."

Lisa sat next to me, crying.

Chuck continued, "Then by some miracle, I made it home in one piece, only to discover Jeannie had a boyfriend. A nice guy too, someone who treated her right." Chuck took a deep breath and continued. "My dad had said 'those are the breaks, son,' so I accepted the news, glad she was happy and thankful I was back home, alive." Chuck folded the paper, put it in his pocket, and then looked at me. "Soon after, I bumped into her sister, who put me in touch with Jeannie. And the rest is history, as they say." Chuck momentarily smiled before his expression grew serious again. "And even though I'm standing here, heartbroken, I feel like the luckiest man alive because I got to marry the woman I dreamed of spending my life with." He wiped the tears that had begun to fall with the palm of his hand. "I just wish we could have had more time together."

There wasn't a dry eye in the crowd, and as the preacher asked if anyone else had something they wanted to say, I stood. I'm not sure exactly what gave me the strength to stand, but I did. Suddenly nervous, I glanced back at Jim, who nodded.

As I stood in front of Jeannie's casket, words came to me. "I loved Jeannie...not just because she was my sister, but because she made me feel like I could handle anything. I mean, all our life she had this crazy belief that no matter what problem came up, I would know how to fix it. Most of the time I had no clue what to do, but knowing she believed in me made me want to do whatever it took to prove her right." I glanced at her for the first time, resting peacefully in her favorite dress, then turned back to my friends and family. "The funny part is that I did always figure out what to do, and she would say, 'I knew you'd fix it, Lou,' and just hearing her say that, and the way she'd look at me. It was like..."

I began sobbing as I thought of her beautiful smile. I couldn't continue and had to return to my seat, where Jim handed me a tissue and put his arm around me. I buried my face in his chest, unconcerned with how loud I cried, and the next thing I knew, we were in line, paying our respects before heading to the cemetery.

As I watched Jeannie's casket being lowered into the ground, I felt a part of me die. Jeannie's faith in me was my greatest strength. Without her, I was weak.

Chapter 37

The month after Jeannie died, I was so depressed I didn't want to get out of bed. But my parents needed me, and there were daily business tasks to handle, so I pushed through. Jim had suggested hiring someone part time so I could focus on family and not have to worry about work, but I was reluctant to give up my responsibilities.

I heard the doorbell ring as I folded laundry. I wasn't expecting anyone, but I saw a man in a brown uniform when I looked through the peephole. He handed me a box from Bernice, which I opened as soon as he left.

I gave her a call. "Thanks for the presents. I love them."

"The scented candle and bubble bath are from me and Alejandro. The tequila is from Juan."

"I had a feeling. Tell him I said thanks." The tequila was one of those hard-to-find brands. I was thankful for the gift but fearful I might guzzle the whole bottle in the hopes I'd feel better.

"How are you holding up?" she asked.

I wanted to lie and say things were getting a little easier each day, but they weren't, and this was Bernice I was talking to. "I miss her," I said. "I keep thinking I might see her around the next corner, but I know I never will."

Bernice sighed. "Life can be so unfair."

"Lung cancer," I said. "Can you believe it? She never smoked a single cigarette."

My thoughts turned to work. "Jim wants to hire someone part time. He thinks I need time to grieve, but I feel like if I stop working, my life won't have meaning, you know?"

"I can see why you might feel that way. But I agree with Jim. If you can afford to take a break, you'd be better off. The work will always be there when you come back."

Bernice was right. It wasn't like I worked for someone else and had to worry about keeping my job. We had our own business and could afford to hire someone for a while.

"Maybe you're right," I told her. "I mean, it's not like I'm going to get fired for leaving."

"Exactly. You're still the boss. Just a boss taking a much-needed break."

After we said goodbye, I put the tequila in the cupboard, lit the candle, and headed to the bathroom with the bubble bath. I filled the tub, immersed myself in the sudsy water, and gazed at the flame. It burned steady at first, then danced from side to side, seeming to have a life of its own. The next thing I knew, I woke up shivering in a dark room, the only illumination an orange dot from the top of the wick that hadn't yet drowned in its wax.

I found a nearby towel and dried off. I climbed into bed and noticed Jim was still awake. I gave him a kiss.

"Did you happen to call the guy to come out and replace the water heater in unit ten?" he asked.

"Shoot. I completely forgot. I'll call first thing in the morning."

Jim turned to me. "Don't worry. I can do it."

I had been forgetting a lot of things. And as much as I wanted to be involved in our business, it wasn't fair to treat the tenants that way.

I snuggled up to Jim. "I was thinking about what you said. About hiring someone part time. I guess it wouldn't be such a bad idea."

He kissed my forehead. "Good. Take some time for yourself. Even if it's just to stay home and read your romance novels and relax."

"And it's only temporary," I added.

"Of course. We'll make sure to say it's a short-term position when we place the ad. That way, there's no confusion."

I felt like a weight had been lifted from my chest after we finished the discussion. Learning to live without Jeannie while helping my parents and having health issues of my own was all I could handle right now. Sometimes even that was too much. As I closed my eyes and drifted off to sleep, I was grateful. The temp worker would be a godsend.

The next day, Jim told me to take it easy, that he and his dad would handle things until they found someone, so I slept late. I lingered over breakfast, read a few chapters of my novel, and made an appointment to get a manicure, something I hadn't done in a long time.

As I studied my reflection in the mirror, I realized I needed to focus more on my appearance. In the midst of everything, I hadn't been bothering to dye my gray roots or apply makeup. That would change starting today, I decided.

"Long time no see," my manicurist said. "How've you been?"

"I've been better." I set my purse down. "My younger sister passed away recently. It was very sudden."

"Oh, honey, that's terrible. Sorry for your loss."

"Thanks."

I selected a polish color then told her about Jeannie's illness as she painted my nails.

"So sad. Especially since she never smoked." She coughed, and from the sound of it, I could tell she did.

"It's a good thing you came here today. You need to treat yourself from time to time." She smiled at me.

"I'm going to be here more often," I assured her. "My husband convinced me to take a break from work. Says we're going to hire a temp."

"I know someone if you're interested."

"Yeah? Who?"

"My daughter, Miranda. She just got a divorce and has been having a hard time. She could really use the money, too."

"What kind of experience does she have?" I asked.

"She used to work in a realtor's office, but now that she's living with me, it's too far away, so she's trying to find something else. Keep her in mind," she said, trying not to seem pushy.

Jim complimented me on my nails when I got home, and I told him about my manicurist's daughter.

"Huh. Well, if she's got realtor's office experience, that's even better. It would save us the trouble of having to put an ad in the paper." He put his hand to his chin, giving it more thought. "But what if she doesn't work out? Wouldn't it be uncomfortable if we had to let her go since she's your friend's daughter?"

"If she doesn't work out, you could just say I'm coming back. That way no one's the wiser if you have to hire someone else."

"Good point. It's settled then. Set up a time for the lady's daughter and me to meet, and then if she seems okay, we have our person."

I nodded, happy I was taking part in company business even while on break.

The next day I called the nail salon and got Miranda's phone number, and after a brief conversation, set up a time for her to meet Jim for an interview. Then I was off to the hair salon to have my hair cut and dyed.

When I came home from the salon, I felt good. The pampering was having a positive effect. I would have to try and convince my mom to get out and do the same. Better yet, I'd bring her with me for a day of luxurious indulgence.

I didn't have a clue how to cheer up my dad, though. Maybe just having Mom in a better mood would make him feel better. And I still had Chuck, Lisa, and Tim to check in on. I wanted to plan something special with them.

I heard Jim come home.

"How was the interview?" I asked as he walked into the kitchen.

"It went well. Sharp kid, around Lisa's age. She'll do fine," he said, then gave me a kiss.

We spent the night talking about current world events, something we hadn't done in a while. Then we made love, another thing we hadn't done in a while, and as I lay on my pillow listening to him snore, I was happy.

***

Dad answered the door when I got to my parents' house.

"You want to come to the nail salon with us?" I joked.

"I think I'll pass. You and your mother go and have a good time."

I didn't need another manicure, but since I was taking my mom for one, I figured I'd get a polish change before we went to lunch.

"Thanks so much for hiring my daughter," my manicurist said. "She's been depressed for a while, and that's the first good thing that's happened to her."

"Happy to help." I handed her a bottle of bright pink polish. "Hopefully, it's the start of a positive trend."

We chatted easily the rest of the visit, my mom sitting next to me with her nail technician, making her own small talk, and when we were done, we headed to a little café for lunch.

Mom set her menu down. "How are you holding up?" she asked me.

"I was just about to ask you the same thing."

Mom exhaled, letting her guard down. "It's hard. A parent never thinks they'll outlive their child." She got a little teary-eyed. "I wouldn't wish the pain on anyone."

"I miss her so much," I said. "I wish she was still here."

The waitress came over, an older lady with a kind face and an updo hairstyle from another era. "Why don't I give you ladies some time, and I'll be back for your order," she said in a soft voice, seeming to understand we were going through something.

We ate our comfort food, which was exactly what we needed. When I dropped Mom off at home, she thanked me for the day out and gave me a big hug and a kiss. "They say time heals all wounds," she said.

"I hope so." I smiled, then waved goodbye, hoping she was right.

Early the next morning, my dad called to tell me my mom had died in her sleep.

I sat, trying to digest the news. Then my heart shattered all over again, into a million un-mendable fragments. She would never have a chance to find out if she was right.

Chapter 38

Mom's funeral was a blur. Unlike Jeannie's, where people got up and spoke, this time no one did. Not because they didn't care or want to honor her, but because everyone was still too shell-shocked from the suddenness of her loss.

I sat in the kitchen staring at a bowl of cereal I couldn't bring myself to eat, then remembered the unopened bottle of tequila in the cupboard. It beckoned me with its promise of dulling my pain, but I decided I didn't want to drown my sorrows in booze and get a headache, so I passed.

I got up and poured my food down the garbage disposal.

First Jeannie, now Mom. It was still so hard to believe.

Jeannie's passing had been devastating, but I had at least gotten time to prepare, however short. With Mom, one day we were having lunch, the next day she was gone. Just like that.

I stared out the window, and it began snowing, small white flakes that hypnotized me, taking me back to the time when Mom, Jeannie, and I made snow angels together in the backyard.

"Do you think there is snow in Heaven?" Jeannie had asked as we lay staring at the sky.

"That's where it comes from," Mom had answered. "But God sends it to us once and a while so we can make angels."

The memory made me smile. Then a cold draft crept in and sent me back to the bedroom, where I hid under a mound of blankets. The scent of Jim's cologne lingered on his pillow, and I pulled it close, thinking how lucky I was to have a husband who took such great care of me. I didn't know when I'd be ready to return to work, but it was nice knowing I didn't have to worry about it.

"We should invite your dad to dinner," Jim suggested after

we finished eating.

I hadn't been over to see him as much as I had planned to. "That's a good idea. Which night?" He and his dad had been putting in long hours lately, repairing a few broken washing machines at the Laundromat and cleaning up one of the units a tenant had trashed before being evicted.

"How about Saturday?"

"Okay. Should I invite your dad, too? He hasn't been over in a while."

"Yeah. That sounds nice."

When I got off the phone with my dad, I realized just how depressed he was and decided to stop by the next day.

Dad looked surprised when he answered the door. "Hey, honey. I didn't know you were coming or I would have straightened up."

"Don't worry," I said as I stepped inside. "It's just me."

The house was a mess, with dirty dishes on the coffee table, socks and shoes left wherever he had taken them off, his coat hanging from the top of the exercise bike. A glance at the curio cabinet told me it hadn't been dusted since Mom had died.

"Are you hungry?" I asked. "I'm in the mood for Luke's and thought you might like to join me."

Dad's face lit up. Luke's was his favorite hot dog stand. "I won't say no to that," he replied, reaching for his coat.

We drove to the restaurant, and after we placed our order, he asked, "Didn't your friend open one of these in New Mexico?"

"Sort of. She was craving Luke's and couldn't get a decent hot dog out there, so she started a chain of her own called Chicago Dogs."

They called our number, and I grabbed our tray, taking it to the counter so we could sit on the stools that had a view of the busy street. Dad and I dug in, and then we nodded at each other, the sound effects we made summing up how much we loved our meal.

We sat and watched the people go by outside when we were finished. I wanted to ask how he was doing but chose not to spoil the moment with conversation. It felt right just to sit together in silence.

Time passed like a slow-moving train. But it was a good kind of slow. After a while, it finally felt right to break the silence.

"Do you want to get chocolate malts to go?" I asked.

"Sure," he said, reaching for his wallet. "Dessert is on me."

By the time we got back to the house, our bellies were on the verge of bursting. Dad eased into his favorite chair, and I sat on the sofa and sighed.

I turned to him and smiled. "I should clean the house to burn off some of these calories."

"You don't have to do that," he said.

"I know, but I want to. If I go home, I'll just end up taking a nap and get fat."

"Well, okay then."

He knew I was trying to help, but we had to play the game first, the one where he acted like he didn't need anyone and I pretended I was doing it for another reason. The truth was we both needed each other, but it wasn't easy to come out and say.

"What are you doing this weekend?" I asked. "I'm having Jim's dad over for dinner on Saturday, and we were hoping you could make it."

"Chuck is taking me to a Bears game tomorrow, but I've got nothing happening on Saturday."

"Okay. Come by at six then."

We made small talk before I started cleaning, and when I was finished, I gave him a big hug before putting on my coat. "Give me a call if you need anything."

"Will do. See you Saturday."

I wished we could have talked about how he was coping without Mom, but my dad had never been one to discuss things like that. Maybe keeping him busy would help. With me stopping by and Chuck taking him to a game, then dinner at our place. Or perhaps Mom was right. Perhaps all he needed was time.

On Saturday, I made a roast with mashed potatoes, a recipe my mom had taught me long ago.

"This is delicious," Dad said.

"Thanks. I remembered it's your favorite."

Jim's dad's plate was almost empty. "I'll have to agree," he chimed in. "I should eat here more often."

"You're welcome anytime," I said, then glanced at my dad. "You, too."

We cleaned our plates and made casual conversation. Afterward, I set out small slices of cheesecake for everyone.

"My ex-wife used to make the best cheesecake," Jim's dad said.

He never talked about Jim's mom.

"If you're still on speaking terms, maybe you can get the recipe for Lou," my dad suggested.

"She died a year ago, so I'm afraid that's not possible."

Stunned, I turned to Jim, but he wouldn't meet my gaze.

"I'm sorry to hear that," my dad said. Then he glanced at me. "Your mom made the best chocolate chip cookies, remember?"

I nodded, still thrown by the news about Jim's mom. "How about I make some soon and drop a batch off by you?" I managed to say.

Dad smiled, and even though I was happy to see it, my mind was preoccupied with trying to figure out why my husband would keep such a huge secret from me.

We headed to the family room afterward and continued chatting. Whenever I tried to catch Jim's eye, he purposefully ignored me. I couldn't wait for everyone to leave so we could talk about it, and he, sensing that, chose to drag their visit out for as long as possible.

When Dad suggested leaving, Jim's dad chimed in that he was tired and had better get going, too. After we said goodbye,

Jim shut the door and turned to face me.

"Before you say anything, I want you to know the reason I didn't tell you is because it wasn't important to me."

I couldn't believe my ears. "How could your mom dying not be important to you?"

"Because we haven't seen each other in years, and after what happened, we haven't had a relationship."

"She's still your mother," I said. Jim rarely disappointed me, and when he did, it was usually over something minor. This was so unlike him. This seemed...cruel.

Jim let out a frustrated sigh. "You don't understand because you and your mom were close. When I heard my mom had passed away, it was like hearing a stranger had died."

I looked down, unable to comprehend how he could have no love for the woman who had raised him.

"This is exactly why I didn't tell you," he explained. "Because I knew you'd react like this and think I should go to her funeral. I didn't want to. What's the point of pretending I cared when I didn't?"

I lifted my face and gave him a stony stare. "Your mom fell in love with someone else. Is that a good enough reason to lose her only child?" I bit my lip, surprised I'd spoken my mind.

"If she loved me, she wouldn't have left," he snapped, his face red with anger.

Jim stormed off, then I heard the bathroom door slam, startling me. I had assumed he was indifferent toward his mom when in reality, he had been crushed. I quietly padded to the bathroom and stood outside. I wanted to apologize but instead listened to him sob for the first time in our entire relationship. The sound broke my heart.

Chapter 39

The next few months were strange. Jim and I never talked about his mom again, but he became unusually distant. I found it hard to believe he could still be upset over what I had said but didn't want to bring the topic up again since it had caused so much trouble. We hadn't argued about anything else, so I couldn't figure out why he was behaving so differently. The few times I had asked if anything was wrong, he replied that everything was fine, which was obviously a lie. If everything was fine, why was he talking to me less and less? Why wasn't he as affectionate?

I called Bernice. "You know how men are," she said. "Just ignore him and stop trying to jump through hoops to find out what's wrong. Go buy some new clothes, and once he sees you not stressing out over his distant behavior, he'll be his old self again."

Her advice sounded good but simplistic. "It just feels like we're disconnected, you know? And part of me is wondering if he's resentful I haven't gone back to work. I mean, he told me to take as much time as I wanted to focus on family, but maybe it's been too long? Maybe he's angry he has to pay someone to do what I used to do?"

"I doubt that."

I sighed. Jim had never been hard to figure out before. We'd always gotten along really well.

"It's just weird that we're not fighting, but it's like he's still mad at me since that night. That's when things seemed to change." I realized I was repeating myself and talking in circles, something I did when frustrated.

"Try what I suggested, and don't give his moods too much attention. It may be that simple," she reiterated.

"Sounds like you speak from experience."

Bernice laughed. "Alejandro isn't always easy to get along with, but I love him. He can be opinionated."

"Which is fine as long as you agree with him," I teased.

We talked for a while longer, and when I hung up, I felt better. I dialed the nail salon to make an appointment and was disappointed to find out my manicurist no longer worked there.

The next day I went shopping for a new dress, then got my nails done by the new lady. When Jim came home from work, I gave him a big smile. "Hey, honey. How was your day?"

"Fine." He gave me a peck on the cheek and looked me up and down. "You look nice," he said. But it was a casual compliment. There was no warmth in his eyes.

"Thanks," I replied, trying to hide my disappointment in his lackluster response. I remembered what Bernice had said, to ignore his mood and continue acting like everything was fine.

We sat down to eat. "I did a little shopping today. I swear, it's been forever since I've bought a new dress. And I went to the nail salon," I said, holding up my hand.

Jim eyed my manicure and nodded approval as he dug into his food.

"But I had to try a new lady because Miranda's mom doesn't work there anymore."

"Really? Miranda didn't mention that," Jim said.

I took a sip of my drink. "Maybe she found a better job."

"Maybe."

Jim and I hadn't talked this much in weeks. Bernice had been right.

Thinking of my manicurist moving on got me thinking of my own situation. "I think I'm ready to come back to work," I said as I stabbed my peas.

The comment hung in the air. I wasn't really sure I was ready, and my delivery echoed the uncertainty.

"Are you sure? Why don't you give yourself more time?"

"I guess I just feel bad that we're paying someone to do something I could do." I paused, trying to put what I was really feeling into words. "And part of me wonders if I got back into my old routine if it might help me move forward. I mean, sometimes being off helps, but a lot of times I wonder if being busy would help even more."

Jim took a drink of his soda, then set the glass down. "First off, you shouldn't feel bad that we're paying someone to help out. We're not paying her much, and she's only part time." He looked me in the eye. "But if you want to come back, I'll let her go. It's your decision. I know she really needs the money, though."

I hated putting someone out of work, especially when I wasn't sure I was ready to return. "Maybe I'll take another month off. Spend more time with Dad." I thought of Miranda again. "Why don't you see if someone else is hiring? Maybe you can help Miranda find a job elsewhere before I return. That way, everyone wins."

Jim studied me with an expression that was hard to make out. "You're a good person, Lou."

I beamed at him and reached for his hand. "You are, too."

We sat on the sofa afterward and watched TV. He sat closer than he had recently but didn't put his arm around me like he used to. I tried not to be upset and stay positive, happy we were making progress, but just thinking that made me sad since our relationship had never been like work before.

That Saturday, Jim had plans with his dad. They were headed to the Chicago Auto Show for a fun father-son day.

Jim eyed the chocolate chip cookies I had baked to bring to my dad. "Can I steal one?" he asked.

"I'll do you one better." I went to the counter and handed him a container. "Here's a batch of your own to go," I said.

Jim gave me a quick kiss. "Thank you." Then he put on his coat and scarf.

"Have fun," I said as he left.

"You, too," he replied as she shut the door.

I checked the time and saw I had a half hour before Lisa

arrived and decided to take a quick nap. She was always so busy but set aside time today to spend with her Aunt Lou and Grandpa. When I closed my eyes, Jeannie came to mind. I thought of her often, but at that moment, it felt like she was right there in the room with me.

Maybe she was.

The doorbell startled me, and I jumped up to answer it. "Hey!" I said, giving Lisa a big hug. "I'll be ready in a minute. I just have to use the bathroom before we leave."

I quickly brushed my teeth so I wouldn't have morning breath, then went to the closet and put on my coat, scarf, and gloves before grabbing the cookies. As Lisa and I walked outside, I noticed a patch of ice. "Be careful. It looks like there's a spot the salt missed."

"Thanks," she said, stepping around it. "I'm so sick of winter. Tim and I are taking a short vacation to the Bahamas in a few weeks. I can't wait."

"Good for you," I said. "That sounds like a good idea right about now."

As we climbed in the car, I thought of Jim and me taking a trip. Maybe that's what we needed. A short tropical vacation so we could reconnect.

On the way to Dad's, I felt upbeat. Lisa had that effect on me. She bubbled with youthful energy.

"How's your dad?" I asked her. I had been worried about Chuck. He was a strong man, but a person could only handle so much.

"He's still having a tough time," she murmured. "But at least today he's out of the house. He and a friend from work went to the car show."

"Too funny. Jim and his dad are there today, too."

Lisa smiled. "Guess it's a man thing. Well, not all men. Tim's not big into cars. He sees them as just a way to get from place to place."

Dad loved cars. I decided to see how long the show was

running and then convince Jim to go again with him. I smiled, knowing that would be an easy sell.

Lisa and I trudged through snow that hadn't been shoveled and rang the doorbell. A few minutes passed, and as we waited, we were hit with several frigid gusts of wind.

Lisa rang the bell again, holding it down longer this time, but there was still no reply.

"You think he remembered we were coming today?" Lisa asked.

"Yeah. I just talked to him last night. He was in the mood for more cookies, so I told him I'd bake some and bring them over. And I told him you were coming."

Dad was getting older but had a great memory. He didn't forget things.

"I'm freezing," Lisa groaned.

I was freezing, too, so I fished my keys out of the bottom of my purse and found the spare one to my parent's house. Once we opened the door, I called out his name because I didn't want him to think we were burglars.

Still no answer.

I figured he must be in the bathroom and headed that way to check. When I turned the corner, I saw my dad lying face down on the floor. I dropped the tin of cookies and ran to him.

"Dad!"

I reached for him, and his skin was like ice. I lifted him halfway so I could see his face. His eyes were open, frozen in a faraway stare.

"Dad! Wake up!" I shook him with strength I didn't usually have, but he wouldn't wake up.

Lisa's boots appeared in my line of vision, and I looked up at her.

"I think I better call 911," she said, her voice shaky, a horrified expression on her face.

We locked eyes. "No...no...no...no...no..." I sobbed.

The ambulance arrived, and two grown men tried to take my

dad from me.

"No!" I shouted. "You can't have him!" They tried to calm me down and convince me to release him, but I wouldn't let go.

Lisa kneeled in front of me. Her eyes were filled with tears. "They just want to help Grandpa. You've got to let them take him so they can help," she said in a soothing voice.

I released him, nodding, and everything went black.

Chapter 40

I never made it to my father's funeral. I just couldn't handle any more loss. I lay in bed, tired and desperately in need of sleep, but every time I'd drift off, I'd see the vacant expression on my father's face and feel afraid.

I got up to use the restroom and caught a glimpse of myself in the mirror. My hair was matted, and I had dark circles under my eyes. I caught a whiff of my body odor and considered showering but just didn't feel up to it. All I could bring myself to do was brush my teeth and lie back down again.

I had finally fallen asleep when I heard Jim come home. He'd been picking up food a lot since Dad died, which I felt bad about but couldn't find the energy to change.

"This is good," I mumbled as I bit into my beef sandwich.

We continued eating in silence. The space between us seemed to grow a little more each day, and I felt powerless to stop it.

"What did you decide on the new building? Do you think it's a good deal?" I asked, trying to start a conversation.

"Too expensive. The guy won't come down in price."

I was full after taking a few bites and wrapped the rest of the sandwich up to have for lunch the next day. "Maybe a better building will come on the market."

"Maybe."

He didn't seem interested in talking, so I found the motivation to take a shower. As I washed my hair, I remembered how I had learned to put on a happy face when I was in pain because people who complained all the time weren't any fun to be around. But I had stopped trying to pretend. I never smiled. I was in a lot of pain, and I was completely useless, both at home and in our family business.

No wonder my husband didn't want to spend time with me.

I didn't even want to spend time with myself.

Bernice called the next day. "How are you feeling?" she asked.

"I feel numb, mostly."

There was a pause. "Have you thought of going to talk to someone?"

"I did, but I didn't want to get involved with the whole analyzing my childhood and taking additional medications crap. I already take enough for RA."

"I just worry about you. You've been through so much in such a short time. It's insane. No one should have to endure so much pain."

"It's been really difficult, but hearing from a friend who cares helps." I didn't want to mention the issue with Jim had gotten worse. Talking about my life was depressing. "How are things with you?" I asked, preferring to hear about hers instead.

"Aunt Grace has been a handful, and the boys are busy doing their own thing. They both have girlfriends now."

I managed a smile. "Those were the days, huh? I've been thinking about them a lot lately, wondering if I could go back in time and change anything, what it would be." I paused, making sure I still felt the same as when I had mulled it over the day before. "The truth is I can't think of anything I would change. I mean, having a debilitating disease and losing the majority of my family wasn't something I had any control over, but the things I did have control over I would have done the same way, so looking back, I have no regrets."

"Most people can't say that, Lou. So in that respect, you are truly blessed."

She was right. I had a lot to be grateful for. It was just hard to see. "Wait," I said. "I just thought of one thing I'd change. I would have taken that trip to New Mexico when we were kids."

"Yeah," Bernice agreed. "It would have been way more fun if you could have come."

Discussing the missed opportunity reminded me of the trip

we never took with Jeannie. A chance we could never get back. "Maybe when I'm feeling better, you and I could go on vacation somewhere."

"Just say when."

When we hung up, I felt the first ray of optimism since Dad died. I pulled the sheets off the bed and threw them in the washing machine, and as I poured the soap in, I realized if I wanted to make this happen, it was up to me.

Lisa came to visit the following week. We hadn't seen each other since the day we found Dad. Since I hadn't gone to the funeral and she went to the Bahamas afterward, it felt like a lifetime had passed.

"Hey, Aunt Lou," she said as I opened the door. She stepped in, smiling and emanating a healthy glow. "I got you a present," she said, lifting a bag so I could see.

"Thank you. That was sweet." I took the bag while she removed her jacket. "Here. Let me get your coat."

She handed it to me, and I hung it up. Then we went into the family room and sat on the sofa.

"Do you want something to drink?" I asked.

"No. I'm good. I want to see you open your gift."

I sat down and picked up the bag, pulled out a small box from within, and popped it open.

"This is gorgeous," I marveled as I lifted the tropical-looking necklace.

Lisa's smile brightened. "The aqua stone is recycled glass, the chain and starfish is vintage-inspired brass, and the little clear stone is a Czech glass bead."

I unhooked the clasp and put it on, getting up and going to the hallway mirror. "I really love it. Thanks so much." I felt a little emotional but did my best to suppress it. I didn't want to cry all the time.

"I brought vacation photos, too." Lisa rummaged through her bag and pulled out an envelope. "Here," she said, thrusting the stack of prints into my hand.

I flipped through the pictures, asking questions about some and smiling at the ones where she and Tim had struck funny poses after having too much to drink. Seeing the two of them happy made me feel happy.

Lisa stayed a little longer, telling me all about her computer programming job and about one of her co-workers who drove her nuts. Most of the time, I just listened as she talked a mile a minute, but I found it soothing. For once, the focus wasn't on me.

"Listen to me. I'm rambling," she said, then glanced at her watch. "I have to run. Tim and I are meeting some friends for dinner." With that, she jumped up. "See you soon."

I walked her to the door and got her coat. "Thanks for stopping by. And thanks for the necklace."

Lisa gave me a kiss on the cheek and waved on her way out, wearing a smile so bright it was contagious. As I watched her car disappear down the street, I prayed she would wear it all the days of her life.

When Jim came home, I was still in a good mood. I had straightened the house and cooked one of his favorite meals. Seeing Lisa's vacation photos got me excited about us maybe taking a trip together.

"Lisa stopped by earlier. She gave me this." I showed him the necklace.

"It's pretty," he said, returning his attention to his food.

We ate for a few minutes in silence.

"They had a great time on vacation," I said, trying to revive the conversation. "Maybe we should take a trip like that? Somewhere tropical. What do you think?"

Jim didn't answer right away. "I don't think it's a good idea," he finally said.

"No? How about somewhere else then?" I didn't much care where we went. I just wanted to go away with him.

I started clearing our empty plates.

"Why don't you sit back down," he said, letting out a heavy

sigh. "We need to talk."

I took a seat, feeling wary.

Jim looked me in the eye, a pained expression on his face. "I don't know the best way to tell you this, so I'm just going to come out and say it: I want a divorce."

I stared at him, unable to believe what he had said. I thought he was going to say money was tight and we'd have to take a vacation next year, or he'd prefer Europe.

Then it sunk in. Our problems were worse than I thought, and I had been too wrapped up in myself to see.

"I know I've been hard to live with lately, being depressed for so long and not working, and I apologize," I said, backpedaling. "It's just been hard losing so many people." The gravity of the situation I was in hit me, and I began shaking. "I never meant to make you feel unimportant. I've always loved you, Jim. You're the love of my life."

"Don't apologize for being depressed. Anyone who has been through what you've been through would be depressed. But look at you, you're pulling through, and all without medication or therapy." He leaned toward me and added, "You're strong, Lou. You can handle anything."

I couldn't understand why he was complimenting me while telling me he wanted to be apart.

"This is just a rough patch," I said. "All couples have them. We had smooth sailing for so many years, and now it's our turn." I took his hand. "We can get through this."

Jim slowly pulled his hand away, lowered his head, and rubbed his forehead. Tension hung in the air, and I held my breath, waiting to hear his reply.

He lifted his head and held my gaze. "We can't get through this, Lou. I didn't know how to tell you this with everything that's been going on, but I have been seeing Miranda. And things have gotten serious."

I sat in my chair, shocked and unable to speak.

"She's pregnant. We're going to have a baby."

Chapter 41

Jim left with a single bag, saying he'd be back on the weekend so we could discuss the details of the divorce after I'd had a chance to calm down. He'd apologized over and over, saying he never meant to hurt me and that he knew the timing was awful. Then he said I was a wonderful person and that he would always love me.

Something inside me snapped when he said that, and I screamed at him to get out.

I paced the apartment, furious. Here I had lost every member of my family, and he was out fooling around with another woman – a girl Lisa's age! And to add insult to injury, I got her the job.

My feet pounded the hardwood floor as I marched back and forth, analyzing the situation in reverse. Jim had suggested I take more time off. He had said there was no rush for me to return to work. I smirked, thinking how at the time I had believed he was so thoughtful.

He had been working late, too. Not enough to where it was suspicious, but in retrospect, it all made sense. He had said he was with his dad all those times. That stopped me.

Did his dad know about this?

Would he approve?

I doubted it, considering what Jim's mom had done to him.

I tried to remember if he had acted differently when he was over for dinner last time. And as I did, I was reminded that Jim had neglected to tell me his own mother had died.

I shook my head. I had felt bad about voicing my opinion on the matter when what I should have been was alarmed. The man was literally full of secrets.

Memories of me lying around looking awful for months on end surfaced. I had been depressed, but I could have showered;

I could have tried to look presentable while grieving the loss of my family.

I sighed in frustration. What was done was done.

Then I thought of Miranda and grew angry. Here I tried to do something good and help a person out when she was in need, and in return, she screwed me over. I'd never even met her, only her mom, who I now wanted to strangle with my bare hands.

I was so worked up I accidentally slammed my shin into the coffee table. "Damn it!" I cursed.

The pain triggered tears that hadn't fallen yet, and I sat on the sofa and sobbed. Jim was the love of my life, and I didn't know how I could live without him.

The thought of him with someone else made me ill.

And they were having a baby!

"What did I do to deserve this?" I cried out. "Why me?"

I had given up on the dream of having a child, and Jim said he had given up on it, too. All he wanted was for us to grow old together.

I sobbed uncontrollably as I realized that I would grow old alone.

The room seemed to shrink, and I had to take a few deep breaths so I wouldn't hyperventilate. Sweating, I got up to get a glass of water. When I stood, I felt light-headed and had to lean against the wall for support.

On the way to the kitchen, I remembered the unopened bottle of tequila. I dug it out of the cupboard and looked for a shot glass. I didn't own one and decided it didn't matter. Today called for a tumbler anyway.

The amber liquid tasted smooth on its way down, just like it had all those years ago at Bernice's wedding. For a split second, I wondered if it was okay to mix alcohol with the painkillers I had just taken. But I quickly dismissed the thought, not caring either way.

I took a second, much larger gulp. And within a short time, I was drunk, fascinated by the intricate design of the label on the half-empty tequila bottle. I considered calling Bernice but chose not to. All I wanted was to feel nothing. To cease to exist.

I thought of the pact Jeannie and I had made when we were kids. Eighty and out, we had said. We were going to leave the planet with dignity.

She had made an early departure. Mom and Dad were gone, and Jim...

Again I thought of him with another woman, smiling and holding their baby, and reached for the tequila and poured the rest of it in the glass, filling it to the rim.

I held it in the air to make a toast. "To a lifetime of happiness for Jim and Lou," I scoffed. A small amount of alcohol spilled onto the table, and I took a sip, dripping some more onto my lap.

As I nursed my drink, I thought of Jeannie, Mom, and Dad. They were the ones who truly loved me, the ones who would never abandon me, no matter what. But they were all gone.

My stomach felt queasy all of a sudden, and I thought I was going to throw up. I lifted the almost empty glass and studied it like it held the answer to a great secret, then set it on the table. I couldn't drink any more. Not a single drop or I'd vomit.

I glanced at my knuckles. Whenever I drank alcohol or ate too much sugar, it would trigger a rheumatic flare, and they were already starting to hurt. Tomorrow's pain was guaranteed to be off the charts.

I stared at my hands, resentful that they had betrayed me, and saw Aunt Violet's instead. I thought of all the times we had gone to visit her at the nursing home and how depressing it was. The only person she had was my mom, her favorite niece, whom she had lavished with all her love and attention.

It had gotten dark outside, and I caught a glimpse of my reflection in the window. What I saw in it terrified me more than anything I had ever seen.

I was just like Aunt Violet.

The revelation was shocking. It was like I'd been slapped across the face by the hand of fate. Frustrated, I whipped the empty tequila bottle across the room and cursed at a God who obviously hated me, then stumbled to the bathroom and stared at myself in the mirror for a long time.

I couldn't be Aunt Violet. I just couldn't.

I reached into the medicine cabinet and pulled out the bottle of painkillers. I swallowed the remaining pills and climbed into bed. I closed my eyes and thought of my sister's dying wish.

"I'm sorry, Jeannie. I hope you will forgive me."

I woke up the next day feeling like shit. I remembered my life was over, and I wasn't even capable of ending it properly. As I got up to use the restroom, I had a vague memory of throwing a bottle across the room and wasn't looking forward to cleaning it up.

I found aspirin in the medicine cabinet and washed a few down with a cup of water from the bathroom sink, and forced myself to take a shower and get dressed. I had things to do. Like clean up the mess I had made and try to figure out what to do with the rest of my miserable life.

When I finished cleaning, I ate a bowl of cereal, climbed onto the sofa, and took a nap. I woke a few hours later, after having a dream of Jeannie and me playing tag as kids, and felt strangely calm.

Jim came by the next day. He looked apprehensive as he came in and took a seat on the couch.

"How are you feeling?" he asked, a concerned look on his face.

"Fine," I replied.

I looked like hell but had made an attempt at fixing my appearance. Not that it mattered since Miranda was twenty years younger and probably glowing with new life from within.

Jim smiled awkwardly. "Good," he said.

He sat up straighter. "I thought it would be simplest if we split things in half. You can have this apartment building, and

I'll take the other. Same thing with the two Laundromats and our bank account."

I still had my parent's house, which was willed to me and paid off.

"Sounds fair," I agreed.

It felt horrible to have this discussion with him. Like a dagger to the heart.

"And what about your father?" I asked. "Doesn't he kind of get screwed in this deal?" It had been their business, and now I was getting half because I was his wife.

Jim's face contorted ever so slightly, and I knew him well enough to know he and his dad hadn't seen eye to eye on this plan.

"Don't worry about him," he said dismissively.

"Oh. Right. He's no longer my concern."

I had planned to be civil but couldn't control my feelings. I really loved Jim's dad and felt it was wrong to "not worry" about him just because Jim had decided to start a new life with someone else.

"I didn't mean it like that," he said. "What I meant is I want to be fair to you."

I crossed my arms and pursed my lips, finding the statement ironic.

Jim's face grew red with embarrassment as he realized how foolish he sounded. He cleared his throat and looked me in the eyes.

"This is hard for me too, you know." His expression softened. "After I got involved with Miranda, I realized it was a mistake, that I was just running away from my problems, and I wanted to break it off so I could try and reconnect with you."

I listened, wondering how he went from being someone trying to correct a mistake to an expectant father.

"But then your mom died, and then your dad, and then due to circumstances beyond our control, we kept drifting apart."

I nodded, accepting partial responsibility, and wished I could go back in time and do things differently. I would have made him a priority. And maybe if I hadn't stopped working, he wouldn't have had to hire someone else.

"Then Miranda got pregnant," he continued. "And I did a lot of thinking." He rubbed his unshaven face with his hand, looking as exhausted as I felt. "I realized I loved her and wanted to be with her, but that I loved you, too, but that I couldn't have you both...so I had to make a choice."

Hearing him say he loved her stung.

"So you decided to leave me for another woman. Just like your mom did to your dad?" I lashed out.

His jaw tensed. "It's not the same," he said.

I laughed sarcastically. "It never is."

Jim bristled. "My mom left me and my dad for another man. I was her son. I should have been the most important person in her life, but I wasn't."

I finally understood his train of thought. "So you're choosing Miranda so you can make your child the focus of your life and be a better parent than your mom was?"

Jim let out a heavy sigh. "Something like that."

I fixed him with a steely gaze. "Then you better get started," I suggested. "There's no time like the present."

Chapter 42

I moved into my parent's house after the divorce. It was dated, but Chuck had offered to help me fix it up. I used a portion of the proceeds from the sale of the apartment building and Laundromat for materials and had set aside some money to pay for repairs.

He had been coming over every Saturday for months, but whenever I tried to pay him, he wouldn't let me.

"C'mon," I said. "You can't just spend your day off working for free. Why won't you let me give you something?"

Chuck wiped sweat from his brow with the back of his hand. "I enjoy doing this stuff." He sat down, taking a break from the porch remodel. "Plus, you've done so much for Lisa through the years. There's no way I'd let you pay me. Not a cent."

My new neighbor, Rhonda, came outside to water her plants. She waved, and I noticed Chuck watching her.

"You should stop by for dinner tonight," I said to her. "I made lasagna, and it's hard to finish a whole tray on my own." She gave me a thumbs-up, and I turned to Chuck. "You're staying for dinner, right?"

"I don't see why not," he said, trying to act casual.

We straightened up outside, and Chuck relaxed in the family room while I heated the food. Then, I heard the doorbell ring and went to answer it. Rhonda came in, carrying a bottle of wine in one hand and a small white cardboard box in the other.

"Hello," she said to Chuck, wearing a big smile. "The place is turning out great. And in such a short time."

"Thanks." Chuck blushed.

I grinned, turning to Rhonda. "What kind of goodies have you got?"

"Leftovers from work. Like you said, I can't eat them all myself. So whatever I don't sell, I either donate to the needy or bring home. I've got a lemon tart, a cupcake, a few cookies."

"Rhonda's a pastry chef and owns her own bakery," I said.

Chuck raised his eyebrows, clearly impressed. We headed to the kitchen and sat down to eat.

I started the conversation but managed to melt into the background as planned, letting Chuck and Rhonda chat. After a few glasses of wine and a couple of hours had passed, it became apparent they had a lot in common.

Once they both had left and I was cleaning up, I smiled. Chuck hadn't shown an interest in anyone since Jeannie died, and Rhonda was recently divorced and shared many of the same qualities as Jeannie.

Later that evening, my thoughts turned to Jim. I hadn't really gotten over him, and I wasn't sure I ever would. Nearly every memory – certainly every significant one – included him. In the few years we had been apart, he had made an effort to stay friends. I tried at first because I didn't want to break the connection, but once his son was born, it hurt too much.

Bernice and I, on the other hand, had always stayed close. I called her the next day to see how she was doing.

"Good," she said. "Not much is new. But I did just read a book that made me think of you. A memoir called *Under the Tuscan Sun*. It's about a lady who goes through something similar to what you did, then moves to Tuscany and finds romance."

I laughed. I had learned long ago that life wasn't like in romance novels. I was about to say so when Bernice asked, "What ever happened to our girl's trip? We always say we're going to go, but we never do."

We never went because everything was always falling apart.

"Are you saying we should go to Tuscany?" I joked.

"I don't see why not."

I had no intention of trying to find romance, but the idea of taking a vacation to a place I had always wanted to visit sounded good.

"Okay," I said. "When do you want to go?"

"Whenever you want to. Like I said, not much is going on."

"Why don't I see if there are any last-minute deals we can take advantage of?"

"Sounds good. Call me back with the info."

I went to the travel agent right after I hung up the phone, feeling like I had to take immediate action. When I returned, I was excited and called Bernice back.

"Book it," she said. "It'll be better if we go together from there, so I'll meet you in Chicago."

"Great! See you in two weeks!"

I rushed to my closet and surveyed my wardrobe. I didn't have anything nice to wear and figured I'd probably need to buy some clothes before I left. I called Lisa after dinner and asked her if she'd go shopping with me.

"Of course," she replied. "This will be fun because it just so happens I need to buy some new clothes, too." She paused, then added, "Maternity clothes."

"Oh my gosh! Congratulations!" I was so excited I began jumping up and down. She and Tim had been trying to have a child, and I was glad it didn't turn into a failed quest like my own.

"Thanks. It looks like you're going to be an aunt again. A great aunt!"

"I'll take it," I said, excited I'd have someone else to spoil.

Lisa and I went to lunch, then to a few stores. She found a few new outfits to get her started and planned to buy more as she grew, but I had a hard time choosing vacation clothes.

"You want to be comfortable but stylish," she said. "I think the reason you're not loving anything you're trying is because the clothing you picked is too…matronly."

I eyed her, surprised by her bluntness. "Well, I am fifty-two years old. I don't want to dress too young."

Lisa nodded. "Maybe we should keep looking." She wandered around the store until she'd found a few new items and handed them to me. After trying them on, I realized they were more flattering and bought them.

I guess I just needed someone to remind me I wasn't elderly, even though it was how I felt.

Bernice told me not to bother picking her up at the airport. She said she would take a cab to my house instead. I had everything packed and had straightened up the house, which was just that moment, finally finished.

Chuck gathered his tools.

"Thanks for all your help. I really appreciate it," I told him. "And thanks for offering to keep an eye on the place while I'm gone."

"No problem. I'll be in the area anyway. Rhonda invited me to dinner next week."

"Well, that sounds just perfect." I smiled, glad my attempt at matchmaking had been successful. "Have a good time."

"You, too. Tell Bernice I said hi."

Chuck left, and I sat on the porch in one of the new rocking chairs and waited for Bernice. I scanned the neighborhood, noticing how much it had changed and how much it had stayed the same. It seemed like yesterday when Jeannie and I played tag in the yard, or I sought solitude in my favorite tree.

I thought of my childhood dream to live out west and marry a man with horses. It hadn't come true, and that was fine. I had grown up and learned that the most important thing was to be grateful for what I had. And the truth was I had a lot. I was financially secure. I had wonderful friends and family, even though I had lost many I loved. And I owned a beautiful house, one that had just been transformed to reflect who I was now but would always make me feel at home because it was where I grew up.

I saw a cab coming down the street and stood up. The car stopped, and Bernice climbed out. I ran toward her, smiling, and gave her a big hug. She had a book in her hand, and I glanced at it, noting it was an English/Italian phrase book.

"I've come prepared," she said, holding it up.

I smirked. She was probably already fluent.

"Good. You're in charge of asking for directions if we get lost."

Bernice and I went inside, and I set her bags down. Then I gave her a tour of the place.

"It's like I always remembered it, only better," she said.

We chatted for a while but went to bed early to wake up on time for our flight.

All the way to Florence, we talked about the stops we'd take on the tour, excited to soon be living the sweet life, or what Italians called *la dolce vita*. Once we landed and were on the way to our hotel, both of us kept saying how beautiful every building was, how we'd never seen anything so gorgeous in our lives.

Our first truly Italian dinner was life-changing.

"Each bite is more delicious than the last," I said. "I've never eaten anything that has tasted so fresh."

Bernice set her wine glass on the table and smiled. "I'm so glad we did this."

My heart was a little heavy that Jeannie couldn't have been with us, but I didn't want to spoil the moment. I smiled. "I'm glad, too."

The week flew by too quickly—a dizzying whirlwind of Renaissance culture filled with museums, churches, and one amazing meal after another. We spent a couple of days in the town of Lucca, a walled city with jaw-dropping medieval architecture. One day, our guide took us on a walking tour, and as Bernice and I moved along, marveling at the red-roofed villas and numerous towers, I was so busy having a good time I didn't even notice my usual arthritis pain.

We stayed at a bed and breakfast in Cortona on the final day. A middle-aged husband and wife ran it, and as we sat down to breakfast, they started having what looked like a heated exchange. Since I didn't speak Italian, I wasn't sure what they were arguing about.

I took a sip of coffee and was surprised when they smiled at each other, and he gave her a passionate kiss on the lips. I turned to Bernice.

"That's Alejandro and me," she joked.

I grinned and stabbed my fork into my omelet, having the time of my life.

While waiting in line at the Florence airport, a distinguished man smiled warmly at me. Bernice noticed and elbowed me, just like we were kids.

"He likes you," she whispered.

"I gathered that," I replied, trying not to giggle.

The man nodded and moved forward in line, then left to board his flight while we checked our bags for our return trip to Chicago.

Bernice turned to me after we were seated on the plane. "I forgot to tell you this. It's kind of funny."

I perked up, in the mood to laugh.

"Alejandro was talking to Juan about us taking the trip to Tuscany, and I guess Juan was a little miffed."

I raised an eyebrow. "How come?"

She smiled and shook her head. "Alejandro told him about the *Under the Tuscan Sun* book, and how the lady ends up finding romance in Italy, and he said Juan seemed jealous."

I started laughing. "You're not serious." Bernice's expression didn't change. "You're not kidding?" I asked in disbelief.

"He said something to the effect of, 'Sure, now she's available after all these years,' and began complaining."

"Boy, that comes as a surprise. I mean, I know he liked me, and to be perfectly honest, I found him attractive too, but didn't you say he's happily married?"

"He's happy," Bernice assured me. "I think he was just gossiping with his brother."

Since my divorce, Juan had apparently thought the same thing I had. That we could have been an item if things were different.

But things weren't different. And that's how life went.

Chapter 43

I had offered to babysit Lisa's daughter, Pam because Lisa had been putting in overtime at work for the end of the year. I kept my eye on Pam as I took my time setting up the Christmas tree. At two and a half years old, she was a handful but a joyous one.

Some claimed the world would end in 2000. And while Lisa worked hard programming to help save it, others stocked up on canned goods and supplies. I, on the other hand, couldn't care less. If the world ended, it ended. If it went on, it went on.

My rheumatoid arthritis had gotten worse, even with the new drugs, and I had given more thought to the pact Jeannie and I made when we were kids. My opinion on it had changed through the years, and for a while, I had thought it was a silly idea, that we had been naïve. Now, I thought we were geniuses and watched the right to die debate with great interest.

I tucked Pam in for her nap and gave her a kiss on the cheek, setting up the village underneath the tree, thinking of my own escape plan. I had botched the attempt when Jim had left but was grateful because it wasn't my time. That was me snapping, unable to take any more loss.

Now, I was sensible. I had lived life, enjoyed it to the best of my ability, and when I turned eighty, I'd end it with dignity as planned. And I'd do it correctly this time. I'd take a whole bottle of painkillers.

I finished decorating the tree and stood, satisfied with how it had turned out. The reality was I probably wouldn't have to do it because studies showed people with RA died younger than people without. The article I had recently read said a decade younger.

The good news was it was my decision. I had control over my own life, no matter what the law said.

I went to the kitchen and made lunch before waking Pam and giving her half of a sandwich with milk. We played with her doll, and then I reached for a brush to fix her hair.

"You want me to braid it?" I asked her.

Pam nodded and turned forward, facing the mirror. I brushed the knots from her hair and began braiding. I stole glances in the mirror as I worked and thought of Jeannie, remembering how I did the same thing to her in the same room all those years ago.

When I was done, Pam smiled. "Pretty," she said, the word sending my heart soaring.

The doorbell rang. It was Lisa.

"Thanks for watching her, Aunt Lou. We've just been so busy. It's like I can't type fast enough." She looked overwhelmed.

"This Y2K thing is scary, huh?"

"Very scary. If the computers aren't fixed, they'll go back to zero when it hits 2000, and it will wreak havoc on every area of our lives."

"Gosh. That does sound bad. Well, you know I enjoy having her, so bring her by anytime."

The new year arrived, and the world didn't end. In fact, it brought me a new neighbor.

"Here. Let me help with the snow," Chuck said after walking over, holding a shovel.

He and Rhonda had just gotten married.

"Thanks." I smiled. "It's nice having you next door now."

Chuck smiled. "Agreed. And I've got to say, I'm really happy."

***

The next few years were some of the best years of my life. Having Chuck and Rhonda next door was fun. Bernice and I had taken a few more vacations. One to Mexico, one to Paris, and a road trip up the California coast. And I got to spend as much time as I wanted with Pam, who was the apple of my eye and favorite person to spoil. I babysat her when Lisa needed me to and watched her once a week in the evening so Lisa and Tim could have a date night.

We had all just had a wonderful Thanksgiving dinner at my house when Bernice called.

"What's wrong?" I asked. "You sound upset."

"I am," she choked.

She began sobbing. "What's the matter?" I asked, alarmed.

"There's been an accident."

My stomach dropped. I prayed she wasn't going to say what I thought she was going to say.

Bernice kept crying.

"Tell me what happened," I said. "Is Alejandro okay?"

"Alejandro's fine." She took a few deep breaths. "It's Juan and his wife. They were hit by a drunk driver."

My heart sank. I was afraid to hear more. "Is Juan okay?" I asked, sick with worry.

"He's in the hospital. He's badly bruised and has a few broken bones."

"Oh, no…"

"It gets worse," Bernice said, continuing to sob. "Juan's wife didn't make it."

I burst into tears. "I'm so sorry," I said. "I don't know what to say."

Bernice and I talked for the rest of the night. The next day, I sent flowers and a get well card to the hospital and had a floral arrangement delivered to the funeral home where the service was to be held. I had considered flying there for the funeral, but it didn't feel right, and after hearing how badly Juan took the loss of his wife, I was glad I hadn't gone.

Shortly afterward, Lisa and Tim went on a road trip, and I babysat Pam. We watched Disney movies all week, and Rhonda came over and baked chocolate chip cookies with us. Pam had been saying she wanted a puppy, so Chuck chased her throughout the backyard while barking, making Rhonda and I laugh, and Pam squeal with delight. We had so much fun. I was sad to see her go home at the end of the week.

Later in the year, Bernice and I were discussing our annual vacation.

"How about the Grand Canyon?" she suggested.

"Too much walking. I'm too antiquated to partake."

Bernice laughed. "How about a spa then? We could go swimming. Get a facial and massages."

"Now you're speaking my language. Being pampered sounds nice."

Bernice knew of several locations, and we discussed which place was best.

"How about you decide this time? You seem to be more knowledgeable in that area." Before hanging up, I asked, "How's Juan?"

"He was really depressed for a while and had to go through some physical therapy, but he's improved."

"Good to hear. All he can really do is take it day by day."

That's how I had done it. Life just kept coming, and I didn't have a choice.

A few days later, I was just walking out the door to meet Lisa and Tim for dinner when the phone rang.

"Hello. May I speak to Louise?" a man said.

"This is Lou."

"Lou, this is Alejandro."

"Hey, Alejandro. What's going on?" He never called me, and I was pleasantly surprised.

"Unfortunately, I have a bit of bad news."

"What's happened?"

Alejandro cleared his throat. "It's Bernice. She had a heart attack."

My legs gave out. I had to steady myself and sit down. "Is she all right?"

"Yes. She's all right. The doctor said it was a minor one. She had some stents put in and is back at home resting." Alejandro's voice quavered, but he didn't break down. "I was thinking if it's possible, maybe you could come and visit soon. I know she would like to have you here."

"Just say when," I told him. "I'm available whenever you think it's best."

Alejandro and I talked for a few minutes more, and we decided I would come in a week or two. When we hung up, I cried, unable to keep it together the way he had, then booked my flight.

I landed in Albuquerque and took a cab to Santa Fe. On the drive north, I stared out my window at the electric blue sky, noting it looked just as vibrant as it did all those years ago. The mountains looked different, though. The many trees that dotted its face were covered with a light dusting of snow, making them seem more majestic.

The car stopped in front of Alejandro and Bernice's place, and I got out. Alejandro came out to greet me and gave me a big hug.

"Thanks for coming, Lou. Bernice is so happy you're here."

"How's she doing?" I asked as he carried my bags.

"Getting better. She's moving around, but I want her to take it slow. You know how she is; she doesn't know how to take it easy."

I smiled. That was Bernice. She had always been that way.

"Well, I'll make sure she does. I promise."

Alejandro smiled and nodded. We stepped into the house, and he put my things in a spare bedroom.

"Let me go check on her. I think she's resting," he said.

I scanned the room as I waited, glancing at the framed family photos on the wall, and then Alejandro returned.

"She's up. Let me bring you to her."

I followed him to their room, and I saw her sitting in bed with pillows propped up behind her.

"Hey, Lou," Bernice said in a small voice. "Thanks for coming."

I went and sat on the bed with her. "You gave me a big scare."

"Tell me about it," she said. "I guess I have to learn to take it easy. Not do so much."

"You're a quick learner. You just have to set your mind to it." I took her hand in mine. "This year's vacation is here. Relaxing at home."

We got caught up, and then she was tired, so I went for a walk outside. Alejandro had run to the grocery store, and I went to take a peek at the horses. Bernice had said they had a black one I might like, a particularly feisty one named Dash.

I found him and looked into his big brown eyes, then stood next to him, admiring his shiny coat.

"He's the one you want to ride if you're looking for adventure," a man said.

I turned and saw Juan. He looked a little older, with a few wrinkles and salt and pepper gray hair, but his warm smile hadn't changed.

I smiled back at him. "I was just looking at him. I wasn't planning on going for a ride."

"Why? Are you chicken?" Juan teased.

I grinned. "I've been through so much in my life. Nothing scares me."

Juan grabbed a nearby saddle and put it on Dash. Then he turned to me and smiled. "Fearless and beautiful, huh?" He reached for my hand to help me up. "Hop on."

Juan mounted Dash, and I wrapped my arms around his waist. The horse exited the barn slowly, but once it saw open land, it began galloping. The rush was more intense than I had remembered it. And as the cool wind blew through my hair, I felt more alive than I had in a long time. The air was cool and crisp, invigorating my every sense as we raced through the foothills.

The rhythm of Dash's breathing reminded me of life itself, and how so many people I knew and loved had died, some of them while still young. I tightened my grip around Juan's waist and rested my cheek on his back.

I had no idea how many more days I had left. All I knew was I wanted every one of them to be like this.

Epilogue

A year later, Juan and I sat next to each other on the porch, watching the sun rise. I glanced at my knuckles before reaching for my coffee. They really did seem less swollen since he had taken me to Chimayo at Christmastime.

"You just have to have faith," he had said as he took my hands in his and smeared them with healing dirt. He closed his eyes and whispered a prayer in Spanish. I kept mine open, marveling at the crutches that hung from the wall inside the church, thinking of the thousands of people who made pilgrimages on Good Friday each year, some walking from as far as Albuquerque.

Juan and I had stayed for the holiday service, and by the time we left, it had gotten dark. The church's exterior had been decorated with rows of luminaria, and all the candles were lit, making the paper lanterns glow from within.

"Merry Christmas," he had said, then gave me a kiss.

I looked over at Juan, his nose buried in the morning paper, and smiled. Then I thought of my last conversation with Jeannie. How she had asked me not to go through with the pact. How she had wanted me to live for her.

I guess in the end, Jeannie got her wish.

And so did I.

The End

Thanks for reading *Eighty and Out.*
I hope you enjoyed it.

Your FREE book is waiting.

The Rescue is the heartwarming story of the dog that cheated death and transformed a woman's life.

Get your free copy at the link below.

Send My Free Book!

To get your free copy, just join my readers' group here:

kimcano.com/the-rescue-giveaway-lp

Books by Kim Cano

Novels:

A Widow Redefined

On The Inside

Eighty and Out

His Secret Life

When the Time Is Right

Novelette:

The Rescue

Short Story Collection:

For Animal Lovers

About the Author

Kim Cano is the author of five women's fiction novels: *A Widow Redefined, On The Inside, Eighty and Out, His Secret Life,* and *When the Time Is Right.* Kim has also written a short story collection called *For Animal Lovers.* 10% of the sale price of that book is donated to the ASPCA® to help homeless pets.

Kim wrote a contemporary romance called *My Dream Man* under the pen name Marie Solka.

Kim lives in the Chicago suburbs with her husband and cat.

Visit her website for a free book and learn of new releases: www.kimcano.com

Find Kim Online:

Website: www.kimcano.com

On Twitter: twitter.com/KimCano2

Facebook Fan Page:
facebook.com/pages/Kim-Cano/401511463198088

Goodreads:
goodreads.com/author/show/5895829.Kim_Cano